COCOA
&
KISSES

COCOA
&
KISSES

•

LAURIE A.
HENDRICKS

AVALON BOOKS
THOMAS BOUREGY AND COMPANY, INC.
401 LAFAYETTE STREET
NEW YORK, NEW YORK 10003

PRINTED IN THE UNITED STATES OF AMERICA
ON ACID-FREE PAPER
BY HADDON CRAFTSMEN, SCRANTON, PENNSYLVANIA

To my beloved husband, Bruce, for believing, no matter what. And to my mother, Margaret Hubbard, for handing down The Fleeting Muse.

Heartfelt thanks to Chris, Wanda, Jane, and Carolyn.

Chapter One

Amanda Roberts eased her red station wagon toward a narrow, one-lane wooden bridge, the icy planks guarded by log railings on either side. Beyond the bridge, she could see that the road bent in an immediate hairpin curve, rendering oncoming traffic invisible.

The gray sky was spitting light snow as she sent up a little prayer that the road ahead was clear, then drove the car onto the bridge. Her foot pumped the brake frantically and her heart pounded when, in a flurry of snow, a large blue Blazer loomed up on the bridge in front of her. It skidded to a halt mere inches from her car, and refused to budge despite the fact that she had entered the bridge first.

With a grumble about rude people, Amanda struggled to put her stubborn gearshift into reverse while the driver of the Blazer honked his horn impatiently.

1

He obviously intended to wait for Amanda to back off the bridge, so he could continue on his way. Just when she thought she had the stick shift under control, the station wagon engine sputtered to a stop.

A moment later, a large man emerged from the Blazer and planted his fur-mittened hands on the hood of her car, staring at her through the windshield. Amanda promptly snapped the lock of her door. The big man grinned, stepped back, and looked at her license plate, shaking his head before he stepped around to her door.

Through the window, Amanda's eyes met the black ones of a copper-skinned man bearing the distinct look of Native Americans who inhabit villages all over Alaska. The weathered creases in his craggy features did nothing to erase obvious good looks enhanced by sharp, high cheekbones. Straight, short black hair was clipped close to his neck and he was bundled into a heavy navy parka.

Amanda rolled her window down a couple of inches. "Can I help you?"

"Yeah, you can move your car. Traffic generally moves one way at a time on a one-lane bridge."

"Traffic generally moves cautiously around blind curves."

"Are you going to move your car? Or shall I?"

Turning the ignition back on gave her an excuse to avoid his penetrating gaze. "I think I can manage by myself, but thank you for your *gallant* offer of assistance—though you were the last one to enter the bridge."

"This is my road and I'm really in a hurry," he stated flatly. "Look, why don't you get out of the car and let me handle that shift? It should be kept in better working order.''

''It works just fine when I don't have someone breathing down my neck,'' she muttered defensively.

The warning glint in the man's eyes hinted the encounter would only grow unpleasant if Amanda continued to defy him. She unbuckled her seat belt, unlocked and opened the door, and stepped out of the car to face him.

''So, this is your road? Are the roads into all Alaskan villages privately owned?''

The stranger's eyes swept over her, as if assessing her worthiness, and she nervously grasped at the tangle of shining red hair whipped across her eyes by a whistling gust of frigid wind. It was obvious he found her lacking. His black eyes danced momentarily as he reached with strong, fur-mittened hands to move her out of the way.

As he slid swiftly onto the seat of the station wagon, she noticed his tight, faded jeans were tucked into odd-looking fur boots with crisscrossed laces. Then wheels spun on ice for a moment, before he expertly backed the car off the bridge and onto the narrow shoulder of the road.

Amanda approached her car as he stepped out and headed back toward his Blazer. It was on the tip of her tongue to offer a polite word of gratitude, but why would she want to thank the man for such high-handed treatment?

Suddenly, he turned and glanced at her dirty California license plate again, then at her stylish pastel-pink ski jacket. He gave a satisfied nod.

''Look, you're probably capable of taking care of

yourself in a Lower Forty-eight city, with all of life's amenities,'' he said in a surprisingly agreeable tone. ''But in the Alaska bush, a lot of self-sufficiency is needed. My advice to you is to turn around here and head for the nearest city where there will be people to take care of you, Princess.'' He spun on his booted heel and walked back to his Blazer.

Amanda gripped the car door frame, her knuckles turning white as she stared, unseeing, at his back. He sounded just like her father. Dad had said almost those same words when she had packed all her precious books and other treasures to go teach in the remote Alaskan Indian village.

At a loss for a smart comeback, she could have kicked herself for the inane words she uttered next. ''I'm not going anywhere, but into Chena.''

Her words caused him to turn around again. Crinkles formed in the brown skin around his eyes and a grin broke across his handsome features. Yet again, his eyes raked her. Now her favorite expensive jeans, tucked neatly into knee-length black leather boots, and her fashionable jacket, purchased especially for this new life in the north country, made her feel conspicuous and foolish. Resentment at his attitude made her raise her chin.

''Sure, Princess,'' the man said with a grin. ''You're heading into an isolated village with a spread-out population of two hundred. Unless you plan to live in the town's only lodge, at a hundred and fifty dollars a night, I hope you have a hammer and nails to build yourself a cabin. Chena is a bush community; it's not a town infested with apartment complexes for restless wanderers. There's no available housing to speak of—''

''I'll manage,'' Amanda interrupted his irritating lecture through gritted teeth. Her green eyes blazed. ''Now, would you kindly move your vehicle so I can be on my way? I do recall that you were in such a terrible hurry. I'd hate to keep you from imposing yourself on your next victim.''

A smile tugged at the weathered lines on the corners of his mouth as he moved toward her, paused, then turned and swung up into his Blazer, slamming the door with a bang. His vehicle shot across the bridge and out of sight down the icy, winding road, leaving Amanda standing in a swirl of snow and exhaust fumes.

Although her knees felt wobbly, she was satisfied she'd had the last word in her unpleasant encounter with the stranger. She stepped back into her car and took a deep, shaky breath to steady her nerves. At least she was secure in the knowledge that, as the new high school teacher in Chena, there was to be a house provided for her. For that reason alone, the stranger's warning about the unavailability of living quarters didn't faze her.

His words may not have bothered you, but his hands sure did, a niggling voice told her. Being grabbed by a stranger on an isolated road would affect anyone's nerves.

But his words *did* bother her. Here she was, more than a thousand miles from home, and her first encounter in the Native American village had to be with a man who, like her father, believed her incapable of taking care of herself. Was she going to have to prove herself to every man who crossed her path? Narrowing her eyes, Amanda relaxed her tight grip on the steering wheel and stuck her chin out in stubborn determination. If she had to, she would prove herself to every man she met. ''No sweat,'' she murmured without conviction.

Did the man live in Chena? If so, wouldn't he be surprised to find her settled cheerfully into a Chena home the next time they had the misfortune to meet? She chuckled smugly and started the car to continue the journey.

The icy dirt road wound like an indecisive snake through the frozen muskeg. Decaying woodsheds, ramshackle huts, and frost-covered log cabins were built on stilts as a defense against the boggy hinterland. Weather-beaten telegraph poles marched like drunken soldiers through the snowy marsh, each leaning warily in a different direction, as if searching for a smoother course through Alaska's frozen interior.

Just as a black, canopied pickup truck passed on the left, Amanda slowed the car to peek through the snow-flecked windshield at a large, varnished log structure on her right. The frost covering the building glittered in the weak sunlight of the winter sky as Amanda read the sign above the wide porch: *Chena School.* A large caribou rack displayed above the hanging sign at the tip of the pointed roof over the porch added a genuine rustic flair.

Since the students were still on vacation, the deserted appearance of her new workplace came as no surprise. Still, the sight of the school caused her heart to leap with anticipation. On the approach to the village, she passed increasing numbers of the sturdy, high-built log cabins she had seen throughout the Yukon and interior Alaska, wisps of smoke creeping from their chimneys.

Rounding a bend, she found herself in the middle of the village. On her right was a typical log building, this time with a sign saying *General Store*. Above it was another prominently displayed rack of caribou antlers.

On the northern edge of an airfield sat the lodge. The inevitable caribou rack was displayed over the simple *Chena Lodge* sign, and Amanda couldn't help smiling at the lack of pretense used in naming the village establishments. She pulled up in front of the long, varnished building to her left where double-paned windows showed hints of red-and-white checked curtains within.

A glance in the rearview mirror caused her to dig in her purse for a comb to tame her windblown locks. Flushed cheeks, thanks to her recent encounter, camouflaged her liberal scattering of freckles.

The pleasing scent of woodsmoke permeated the village, and trees that had lost their leaves made a dark tracery of bare branches against the winter landscape. With mincing steps, she carefully crossed the icy area in front of the lodge, passing the white patrol car of a state trooper parked neatly beside a battered brown pickup. When she pushed open the heavy log door, she was greeted by a rush of warm air and the curious stares of locals.

Seating herself at a table that looked out over the airfield, Amanda thought they looked like an unusual assortment of people. A wizened Native American man with a mass of silver hair was in animated discussion with a red-bearded fellow wearing a bright, old stocking cap. Next to them, the state trooper grinned boyishly at Amanda from under a mop of curly blond hair. A hefty, middle-aged Native American woman wearing fuzzy purple slippers laboriously pulled herself up from her chair and shuffled over to Amanda.

"Need a menu?"

Amanda smiled. "No, thank you. Just a hamburger and coffee."

The woman eyed her slim figure with disapproval before grunting and shuffling out of sight into the kitchen. When she returned with a cup of strong black coffee, Amanda ventured a question. "Do you know where I might find Mr. Kincaid Russell?"

Heavy dark brows rose as the woman looked at Amanda with renewed curiosity. The conversation across the room ceased as Amanda again found herself the center of interest.

"You a friend of Kin's?" the woman asked warmly.

"No, I'm going to be teaching school here, and I understand he owns the house I'm supposed to rent. My name is Amanda Roberts." She took note of the woman's softened expression and stifled a grin. Her romantic heart wondered tenderly if her waitress had more than a passing interest in her new landlord.

The hostess waved a hand in the direction of the occupied table near the kitchen. "I'm Elly, and that's my husband, Billy, with the red hair and stupid hat."

The men in the corner looked flustered, as if they had suddenly been spotlighted on a stage. They promptly turned away to resume their lively conversation.

Elly nodded toward the chattering old Indian and continued. "That's James Wolf. Trooper Paul Donaldson works out of the station on the highway, about ten miles back."

Amanda sipped her coffee and tried to bring the friendly woman back to her main question. "Where did you say I have to look for Mr. Russell, Elly?"

Elly's ample form jiggled with her chuckle. "Just about everywhere! Kin's always on the go." She shook her head and sighed heavily. "That boy's buried himself in work for years, ever since a woman from Outside broke his poor, big heart. You know," she continued, shaking a sausage-like finger at Amanda, "he can be hard on a tenderfoot, but don't you pay him no mind."

"I see," Amanda uttered with faint hope. Her new landlord sounded like another man she'd met today. Was the village full of narrow-minded men? And would she ever locate the elusive Mr. Russell through her talkative hostess? "He's a busy man, then." She'd originally assumed he would be an old, retired man with time on his hands to do repairs, collect rent, and, maybe, romance Elly. But if he was nursing a broken heart, the latter, certainly, was unlikely.

"Busy!" The woman practically barked with laughter. "Kin's our local boy that done good for hisself. He went away to college and learned how to run businesses. Then he came home and built the lodge and bought the bar out back. That boy wrote up a whole new set of rules for the bar and is real strict about it. Billy and me run the lodge for him. Kin's in

Tok on business today, but he'll be back later. Tok's real close, just down the road a piece, maybe fifty miles or so.''

As Elly paused for breath, Amanda asked quickly, "Do you know where the rental house is?"

The woman's round face registered surprise. "Sure, everybody knows the house Kin rents to temporary teachers. It's that little A-frame just across the road. Well, I'd better go check on your burger."

Temporary teachers? Surely she had misunderstood the woman. Amanda quelled the flutter of panic that arose in her chest. It had been her understanding that this was a permanent teaching position. She was so proud of this move and so excited about a whole new way of living, it would be devastating to find out they only wanted her for a short time. No, she wouldn't think like that. The job was hers for as long as she wanted it and her hostess simply wasn't clear about things, she decided.

Curious, Amanda got up and walked over to the window to look at the A-frame. She was surprised she hadn't noticed it before. It was a brown wooden building, its only distinguishing characteristic being its A-frame style in this village of log cabins and huts. A chimney rose at one side of the building and a picture of a cozy fireplace entered her mind.

Elly emerged from the kitchen with her meal as she returned to her table. The Native American woman set a large cheeseburger and potato salad on the table in front of Amanda. "Some people don't eat enough to keep a muskrat alive," she grumbled. "You eat that salad, y'hear? I won't have people slipping out of Chena Lodge with growling bellies." She looked down at Amanda, concern evident in her dark eyes. "I bet you're tired after your trip, honey. I know Kin'd want us to set you up in one of the rooms till he gets back. He's so thoughtful and generous, that boy."

Elly spoke with what Amanda thought was almost reverence. Kincaid Russell must be the patriarch of Chena.

"That would be nice. It's been a long trip north."

Elly waved a hand toward a door opening onto a hall. "When you're done eatin', I'll put you in a room."

Amanda surmised the lodge's accommodations lay that way, and looked forward to a shower, a session with a good book, and a nap before she met her new landlord. She attacked her meal with gusto.

A short time later she had finished her lunch and nibbled on a pickle while watching a small plane make a careful landing on the slippery airstrip. Someone approached her table, and she turned to look up slowly. First, she saw a sidearm and ammunition attached to a wide, black leather belt. Then a gold badge gleamed on a dark, heavy parka, before she found bright blue eyes watching her out of a smiling face. A dark Smokey-the-Bear-type hat was in gloved hands and the open, energetic look on the man's face was so at odds with the uniform and official stature, Amanda could not refrain from returning the smile.

The trooper removed his gloves and held out a hand. "Hello, Miss Roberts. I'm Paul Donaldson of the Alaska State Troopers' station out on the Alcan. I hear you're the new teacher. Welcome to Chena."

Amanda shook his hand. "It's always nice to know

the local law enforcement.'' She motioned to the seat across from her. "Please, sit down.''

He removed his parka, tossed it over the back of a chair, and sat. "Elly says you'll be renting Kin's A-frame.''

Remembering the stranger's dire warning about scarcity of housing, Amanda shifted nervously. "Well, yes, that's the plan. But she said he rents it to temporary teachers and I'm not temporary. Do I need to find another place?''

Paul smiled. "Don't take that comment so seriously. Elly speaks from the experience of seeing a lot of teachers come and go in a short period of time. She thinks all newcomers are temporary. Chena has to grow on you. A lot of teachers from Outside don't want it to grow on them once they see it. We hope you won't feel the way your predecessor did.'' His smile was one of resignation. "We hope you'll stick around a while.''

"I'm not sure what you mean by outside teachers . . .'' she said hesitantly.

"In Alaska, 'Outside' means the Lower Forty-eight.''

"I get it. And what do you call Hawaii?'' she asked with an impish grin.

He laughed heartily. "We call it Hawaii.''

Amanda joined his laughter and felt a sense of relief that at least one man in town was pleasant company. The stranger she'd met on the road could take a lesson in friendliness from Paul Donaldson.

She sipped her coffee. "Have you lived in Chena long?''

"I've been out here a year and a half.''

"I suppose things are pretty quiet as far as the law enforcement business goes."

Paul shook his head. "You'd be surprised. We're near the Canadian border and there's always some kind of action out there. Some big drug busts go down, so we get called out there to pick up criminals periodically."

Amanda's fertile imagination conjured up pictures of drugs and fugitives running amok through the picturesque, snow-draped village. It didn't seem possible. "Well, surely Chena itself doesn't have that kind of trouble. It's so tiny and quiet."

"For the most part. But we've got our share of problems. The tribe has placed pretty strict liquor laws on the village. You can't buy alcohol by the bottle here and the one bar in town is only open on Friday nights. Kin's real strict about alcohol."

"Is Mr. Russell the mayor of Chena or something?" Amanda wasn't sure whether it would be a blessing or a hindrance to have a local hero as a landlord.

Paul chuckled, pushed back his chair, and stood. "No, Chena doesn't have a mayor. Only a chief. But Kin is loved and respected around here." He picked up his coat and put it on. "He's helped the tribe and this village a lot. People value his ideas and opinions," he added, tugging on his gloves.

"Is he a member of the tribe?"

"He's Athabascan. You're lucky to have him as a landlord. He keeps all his places in good repair." Donaldson placed his hat squarely on his head and zipped his parka. "I'd better get back to the station. Call if you need help with anything. Things can come up, you know. Especially for a cheechako.'' Catching her frown of confusion, he looked sheepish. ''A newcomer.'' He waved to his other companions and went out the door into the gathering afternoon dusk.

Elly soon escorted Amanda down a wide hallway with creaking wood floors covered by indoor-outdoor carpet. She unlocked the black wrought-iron latch of one of the doors about halfway down the hall and Amanda followed her into the rustic room.

The setting afternoon sun shone weakly through the window. On the knotty pine wall above the bed hung a watercolor of several black bears fishing for their dinner in a rushing river. Nightstands on each side of the double bed boasted lamps of knotted birch log with shades of stretched animal hide.

Elly checked the bathroom to see that all was in order. ''All the rooms have different floor plans or color schemes. Kin's traveled Outside and that boy just hates a typical motel room. He says character is important in everything.'' As she turned on a bedside lamp, a warm glow camouflaged the meager light offered by the setting sun. ''Now you just rest. I'll bring you a snack in a couple of hours, and when Kin shows up, I'll tell him you're here. Don't think he was expectin' you today.''

As they headed back down the hall, the friendly woman bubbled on. ''Things'll be real quiet for you 'cause we don't have any guests at this time of year. Folks don't hang around this part of Alaska much in winter,'' she said with a puzzled shake of her head. ''Word gets out that it's a bit chilly, I guess.''

Amanda suppressed a grin at the extreme understatement and thanked Elly. She then zipped her ski jacket before braving the subzero elements to collect a tote bag and a few other items from her car.

A warm shower relaxed her before she closed the blue gingham curtains against the cold, dark winter afternoon. Wearing a floor-length red robe, she snuggled under the bed covers with a mystery, but instead of reading, found herself reflecting on all she had learned about the Athabascan village in the short time since her encounter with the stranger on the Chena road. Both her father and that disturbingly handsome man would see what she was made of.

Thoughts and visions of a dark, weathered face and obsidian eyes made her toss and turn before she succumbed to the dreamlike images. Worn out by the long trip north, she finally fell into a deep slumber.

Several sharp raps on the thick birch door of her room awoke Amanda. She recalled Elly's crusade to fatten her up, smiled, and padded barefoot across the room to open the door. The cheerful smile faded as she found herself face-to-face with the stranger she had met on the Chena road a few hours earlier.

Chapter Two

The navy down parka had been removed and she noticed he wore a woolen plaid shirt with his faded jeans and wry grin. He leaned casually against the doorjamb, one booted foot crossed over the other.

Those ever-appraising black eyes took in the tousled hair that tumbled about her shoulders. Amanda stared back while her nervous fingers toyed with the folds of her robe. "Have I left my car in another inconvenient place?"

His grin was lazy. "I hope not." He crossed his arms over his broad chest. "So you're Amanda Roberts, the new schoolteacher? I should have known. Should be an interesting semester coming up. It's not often Chena gets a Macy's fashion princess for a teacher."

Amanda's hands balled into fists at her sides while her temper simmered just below the boiling point.

16

This man had learned fast how to push all the wrong buttons. It was as if her father had phoned ahead to pass on to this new nemesis the exact information about how to treat his twenty-four-year-old daughter like a child.

"Yes, I'm the new teacher. And are you one of the children I'll be teaching?" She tapped a neatly trimmed fingernail against her lips and appeared to consider him seriously. "But, no, you couldn't be. I'm teaching high school and you don't seem quite mature enough."

Was that a glimmer of laughter in those inscrutable eyes? But it was gone in a flash, and she decided she must have been mistaken. The satisfied smirk he wore should have warned her what was coming next.

"No. I'm your new landlord, Kincaid Russell."

Amanda's mouth dropped open. She felt as if she'd been hit in the face with a wet rag. What a prospect! This macho male was the owner of the house she was supposed to rent? And he was the owner of this lodge and the bar, too? *He* was the hero of Chena? Well, she'd just have to make other living arrangements, that's all. She'd show him she wasn't some "fashion princess" above pounding the icy roads of Chena in search of a better place to live than his stupid A-frame.

Ignoring his crooked grin, she snapped her mouth shut and prepared to give him a good set-down. Her tone was coldly civil. "I'm not sure I'll be renting your house yet, Mr. Russell. I plan to view all available places in the area before I sign a lease anywhere."

His eyes twinkled with an assurance that made her bristle.

"Naturally. So, when would you like to move into my house?"

Hands on hips, she frowned. "I said I plan—"

"To view whatever is available, yes, I know." He waved an impatient hand. "Well, my house is what's available. That is, unless you plan to commute from Tok every day. It's about fifty miles one way, so I guess that would be a commute of only a hundred miles a day."

He appeared to consider his next words. "Of course, the road conditions usually leave a lot to be desired," he said, watching her closely. "There are our long, hard winters with icy conditions, followed by a couple of months of slow, dusty summer construction work to repair the winter damage. Then winter is back again."

It was obvious he was trying to scare her away. But it wasn't going to work. No way was she *ever* going to admit defeat out here in the bush. She'd never live it down back home. "Are you telling me that there is absolutely no other housing around here?"

"I told you earlier," he drawled, "there's no housing here unless you plan to build your own." His eyes rested on her well-manicured hands. "I wouldn't recommend the Alaska bush in the dead of winter to start your first attempt at construction."

Tucking her fingers into the pockets of her robe, Amanda silently conceded defeat on the question of housing. She would simply adjust to having the perverse Kincaid Russell as her landlord. Paul Donaldson

said Russell kept his properties in good repair, and
that was all that really mattered to a renter. He was
simply the first big hurdle in her bid for indepen-
dence. Well, maybe the second hurdle, after her father. Still, she had no intention of allowing him to
think for one minute that the idea of renting from him
held any appeal.

"Well, if that's how it is, I guess we'll both just
have to live with it." One hand inadvertently touched
her aching clenched jaw.

His mouth twitched with humor. "I'm under-
whelmed by your enthusiasm." Reverting to a busi-
nesslike attitude, he stood away from the door. "I
have time now to take you to the house if you'd like
to start settling in. Unless you'd prefer to stay in the
lodge tonight and move in tomorrow?"

It was best to finish with the formalities so she
could be rid of him. Then she wouldn't have to deal
with him any longer than necessary. "No. I'd like to
see the house now."

With one sweeping arm, he motioned down the
hall. "I'm ready when you are."

She couldn't quite contain her irritability. "Would
you mind terribly if I changed into something more
presentable before we go outside?"

He grinned. "You look fine to me."

Amanda gave him a baleful stare, shook her head,
and drew back to close the door in his face. She heard
him laugh and call out to her that he'd wait in the
dining room.

The short walk across the road to the A-frame was
accomplished in silence while Amanda feigned intense interest in her rustic surroundings. An inner

voice told her she wasn't fooling her companion one bit. Despite the hour, it was dark and the solitary street lamp lit only the tiny center of Chena, so there wasn't really anything to look at.

Kincaid unlocked the door of the house and politely stood aside to allow her to enter. He flicked on a light switch and closed out the cold afternoon air with a push of the door.

Crossing his arms, he surveyed their surroundings with pride. "As you can see, the house consists of one and a half levels."

Amanda headed for the kitchen as he talked. The warmth and character of the place enchanted her. He told her that the upper level was a loft consisting of the master bedroom and bathroom.

"There's another bedroom and bathroom down here," he explained.

"Two bathrooms in this small house," Amanda murmured.

"Yes, we found a way to incorporate the outhouses a few years back by just adding modern plumbing. Amazing, huh? It was a big day for Chena."

Amanda gave him a withering look and walked past him to admire the living room onto which the front door opened. The wall slanted upward to the peaked ceiling and the house was fully carpeted and furnished. The furnishings faced a wood-burning Franklin stove near a stone inset on the knotty-pine wall.

After peeking into the downstairs bedroom, she headed for the open stairway to the loft. Her hand trailed along the smooth banister as she climbed the plush carpeted stairs.

The cozy loft bedroom had one window and she envisioned herself reading in bed and watching the snow fall softly outside. She walked back to the balcony to observe Kincaid. He stood with his back to her, staring silently out the window. His six-foot frame was powerfully built and Amanda guessed he was about thirty. The rustic surroundings fit him, yet she instinctively felt he would be just as comfortable in a major metropolis. He was overendowed with self-assurance and good looks, she thought as she started down the wide stairwell.

The smooth sole of her dress boot slipped on the carpet of the bottom step at the same time Kin turned to face her. Seething with embarrassment, she grabbed the newel post to steady herself.

"Are you all right, Princess?"

She strove to control a racing pulse and keep her voice from shaking. "Y . . . yes. Thank you."

There was a low rumble of laughter in his throat when he spoke. "Seems you need to learn to negotiate stairs as well as bridges."

Amanda bit back a comment about road hogs before releasing the railing. "I'll have a look at the lease now, if it's ready to sign." Seating herself on the couch, she primly folded sweaty hands in her lap. It wouldn't do at all to have him think she found him attractive.

He followed her to the overstuffed couch. "There is no lease. People tend to discover all too quickly that life in the bush isn't to their liking. It's isolated. It's bitter cold in the winter and an armpit in the summer. The mosquitoes drive many Outsiders stark, raving mad. The nearest major city is four hundred miles, whether it's Anchorage to the southwest or Fairbanks to the northwest.'' Pointedly, he eyed her trim pastel jacket and expensive jeans. ''You won't find any shopping malls around here, Princess. I don't expect you'll be here long enough to fulfill any lease I could dream up.''

His words stung more than she wanted to admit. He'd only just met her and already he had decided she was unreliable. ''Are you finished with your lecture on the ills of the bush, obviously worded in an attempt to make me turn tail and run? Because if you are, I'd like to start getting settled. Here, in Chena, in the bush, with all the cold, and heat, and mosquitoes, and solitary general store. Some people enjoy new challenges and adventures.''

Bafflement and irritation at her open hostility marred her new landlord's face. If what Elly had told her about his past hurts could be believed, she was surprised that he took her anger in offense. Still, she wasn't through enlightening him. ''Some people like experiencing ways of life different from their own. And I don't scare easily. Your attempt at turning Chena into a little village of horrors for me leaves a lot to be desired. Your attempts to scare me off won't work. I'm not going anywhere.''

''Most people think they like such things until they come face-to-face with brutal reality,'' Kincaid said seriously. ''People come here expecting to play with the bears and moose and teach the ignorant Indians how to read and write. You'll be gone by the end of the semester, just like all your predecessors. The school will be lucky if you even last that long.

''I'm just trying to warn you that this place is un-

like any you've ever known, and you won't be able
to hack it. You'd be better off cutting your losses now
rather than later.''

He stood and headed for the door, but Amanda
wasn't about to let him get away with that crack.
''Just who do you think you are?'' She was gratified
to see him turn around in surprise at the heated anger
in her voice. ''If you know everything, why aren't
you teaching the kids *you* refer to as 'ignorant Indians,' instead of turning yourself into a little Caesar in
this village? And if I want to leave at the end of the
semester, that's my business. If I choose to stay
twenty years, that's my business, too. Neither you nor
anybody else has anything to say about it. But I give
you my word on one count,'' she said fiercely. ''I
won't leave this village before my contract is up, if
only to prove you wrong.'' She suddenly ran out of
steam and watched him warily, unsure what his next
move would be.

Kincaid Russell regarded her through veiled eyes
for a few silent seconds, shrugged, and turned back
to the door. ''You can move in any time,'' he said
tonelessly. ''There are two keys on the kitchen
counter. Don't worry about the rent. You can start
paying next month.''

With that parting message, he was out the door,
leaving a speechless Amanda staring after him, feeling ridiculously let down. One minute he was ha-
ranguing her about daring to come to Chena and the
next he was giving her a couple of weeks rent-free.
This last act of his blew sky high her opinion that he
was just a greedy businessman out for every dollar he
could get in the village. She shook her head ruefully

to chase away the inconceivable idea that he might have a decent streak, after all.

Still, she didn't need or want to be around a man who had the same low opinion of her capabilities as her father. Dad was wonderful, and they had always been close, but his inability to believe in her competency to manage on her own had always been a sore spot. When she had announced in no uncertain terms that she was going to teach in Chena, come hail or high snowbanks, they'd had a shouting match. He was determined to keep her wrapped in cotton batting until he could hand her gently over to a husband who would be sure to treat her the same way. In the end, he'd told her he would refrain from saying "I told you so" when she came home in a few weeks, after realizing that he was right, and the Alaska bush was no place for a city woman on her own.

The loud buzz of a snowmobile going past on the street outside brought her up short. If she was going to move in tonight and still be rested up from her trip before the reopening of school in a few days, she'd better get moving. There would be time to brood for the rest of her life if she chose. She headed quickly out the door and into the cold, dark afternoon to get her car and belongings from the lodge.

Elly was playing checkers with her husband in the lodge restaurant when Amanda tried to pay for the use of the room. The woman adamantly refused to accept her money.

"Mr. Kin would skin me like one of them caribou he's so fond of huntin'," Elly told her emphatically. "He left orders to make you comfy if you arrived any time he wasn't around. That's what I did. I follow orders and that's that.'' She swatted a beefy hand at her husband as he jumped one of her kings. ''Now, git, Missy. You're makin' me lose.''

Amanda was struggling to move heavy boxes into her house when she noticed two village men approach on foot. One was an Athabascan and the other a muscular, bearded fellow. Since she expected them to continue on to the general store, she was surprised when the Athabascan took a heavy box of books from her and carried it into the house. As she turned, the other man hefted another box from the car and followed his companion. Grabbing clothes from where they hung on hooks in the car, she quickly followed the men, only to pass them as they exited the house and headed out to pick up more boxes.

Bewildered, she trailed behind them with her load of clothes. ''What's going on?'' The men remained silent, and she followed them back into the house again, this time remembering to place the clothes over the back of a chair. The Athabascan left a load in the living room while his friend set a box on the kitchen counter. Then they walked stoically around her to go back out the door. ''Excuse me.'' She followed them to the tailgate and planted herself firmly in their path.

''I'd just like to know who you are and why—'' She threw her hands up in despair as they moved around her with their next load. ''If I sat on the tailgate, they'd still get around me and not say 'boo'.'' If they heard her muttered comment, they gave no sign. So she shrugged in resignation and decided to be thankful for their help, gathering more clothes and nodding her head in greeting when she passed her two single-minded helpers.

The last item to be brought into the house was an old, half-bald, lime-green stuffed hippo with a ragged red ribbon around his neck. Amanda hurried to take her precious Hailey Hippo from the bearded man, who eyed it dubiously. She then closed the door and stood with her back against it, trapping her silent assistants. She gave them a mischievous smile. "And just who are the two gentlemen I can thank?"

"I am Joseph James and this is Kirk," the Athabascan said gravely. "Kincaid sent us to help you. You may thank him."

"Well, Joseph and Kirk, I'm grateful to both of you. Can I make some coffee? I know which box holds the right stuff." She pointed to a particular grouping of boxes.

Joseph motioned for his friend to follow him to the door. "No. Gotta go. Things to do."

Knowing from experience that these men let no obstacle stand in their way, Amanda moved quickly aside, pulling open the door as she did so. "Thanks again, fellas," she called with a friendly wave as they disappeared into the cold evening.

Amanda smiled and considered Joseph's explanation as she closed the door against the darkness. Kincaid Russell was certainly an enigma. He as much as told her she was an incompetent female, then sent men to help her unload her car to underline his opinion. Still, she found it hard to be angry about that because, in her own mind, such an action was one of kindness and gallantry, rather than an insult.

And then there was the other facet of their new

acquaintance. He was the most interesting and attractive man it had ever been her pleasure to encounter. If only he didn't have such a prejudice against Outsiders.

With a gusty sigh, she pulled off her coat and tackled the box Kirk had set on the kitchen counter. The action reminded her that Kincaid said he'd left two keys there, yet there was only one next to the box. Lifting it, she looked underneath, but the extra key wasn't there. Dropping to her hands and knees, she examined the carpet in front of the counter and checked under the bar stools. No spare key. With a shrug, she made a mental note to talk to Kincaid about it, and set back to work.

The next afternoon, Amanda walked over to the general store and received an unplanned lesson in the meaning of the word "expensive." A gallon of milk was more than five dollars, and a loaf of bread cost half the price of the milk.

She placed a basket of provisions on the worn Formica checkout counter, saying to the cashier, "I seem to have taken the last gallon of milk off the shelf."

The pretty young Athabascan woman, glossy black hair cascading down her back, smiled and rang up Amanda's purchases on an old-fashioned cash register. "That's okay. Supplies come in the day after tomorrow."

Amanda's jaw dropped in astonishment. "You mean you don't have a stockroom?" Her hand waved vaguely toward the back of the store. "I actually took the last gallon of milk in the whole town?"

The woman pulled a cardboard box from a stack

behind her and set it on the counter. "We have a stockroom for nonperishables, but we can't keep a lot of fresh stuff. Supplies come two days a week, same days as the mail truck, so it's not much of a problem. You'll get used to it in no time at all." She turned a box of cereal over to read the price tag. "You're the new teacher from Outside, aren't you?"

Of course, it was natural that word of her arrival had already spread in the tiny village, so Amanda responded without surprise. "Yes."

The smiling clerk placed her purchases in the box. "My name's Vanessa, but everyone calls me Van. While you're in Chena, just remember to buy plenty of anything you use a lot of when supplies come in on Monday and Thursday. Kin does his best to order the right amount of everything for the village population. But sometimes it's hard figuring how much to order, so we do have shortages occasionally." She chuckled. "This is the kind of town where neighbors really do ask to borrow a cup of sugar once in a while."

The idea left Amanda feeling slightly bemused, but something else the clerk had said caused her antennae to twitch. "So, Kincaid Russell works here?"

Just then, the door behind Amanda opened and the clerk looked up with a broad grin. "Yeah, Kin does a little work now and then, just to keep up appearances, since he owns the place."

At the woman's satisfied giggle, Amanda turned and saw Kincaid Russell. She caught her breath at the sight of him clad in jeans, a fur parka, mukluks, and black leather gloves. Such rugged good looks ought to be illegal! Then recalling her pride, she nodded shortly and turned her back on him to pay the cashier.

Kin approached the counter next to her and addressed the clerk as she handed Amanda her change. "Hello, Van. I see you two have met."

Amanda, whose heart had inexplicably fallen to her stomach with a thud when he kissed the clerk, fumbled with the change, sending it spilling to the floor as she tried to stuff it into her wallet.

A knowing grin lit Kin's handsome face and he joined her when she knelt to retrieve the money. "I saw your car at the house. I guess you'll need some assistance getting your supplies home." He placed some of the delinquent cash in her hand, his fingers brushing hers briefly.

Feeling her hand go weak, Amanda gripped the money in a tight fist. "I'll be just fine on my own." She stuffed the money into her wallet and stood, hoping the heat that suffused her face wasn't as evident as it felt. "I don't need a car or anything else to carry a few little groceries a couple of hundred yards to the house."

In an effort of defiance, she hoisted the box containing her groceries off the counter. An unwilling grunt escaped her at the surprising weight, but she still attempted to move awkwardly around him to the door.

He stepped in front of her and deftly took the heavy box, tucking it under one arm. "Don't be silly. You won't last a week in the bush if you don't learn to accept help from people. And it's pretty obvious that you need a lot of help." He opened the door with ease and let in a frigid blast of winter air.

Pinning him with an equally frigid stare, Amanda stalked past and headed toward the A-frame. The knowledge that she'd overreacted to his criticism didn't make it any easier to remain calm. His attitude infuriated her even more when he quickly caught up with her while she slowly picked her way across a particularly nasty patch of ice.

He was able to move across the snow and ice as if he had suction cups attached to his feet. She idly wondered if that might be the case, or if maybe he had spikes on the bottoms of his boots. Her eyes drifted downward in search of such evidence, but there were no visible attachments on his feet. Unable to stifle a giggle at her own fancy, she elicited a puzzled frown from the man walking beside her.

He must really think I'm crazy. Well, maybe that's good. Maybe if he thinks I'm crazy, he'll leave me alone. Somehow, that idea wasn't at all appealing. It gave her the same unwelcome, heartsick feeling she had experienced when he'd kissed the clerk in the general store.

Maybe graciousness was the best policy. "Thank you for sending Joseph and Kirk to help me unload my car yesterday."

He entered the house and deposited the grocery box on the kitchen counter before turning toward her. "They were bored. It kept them out of trouble." His tone implied that sending the men to help her was of the utmost insignificance.

She placed the perishables in the refrigerator. "Is keeping law and order another of your duties?"

"Despite the presence of the troopers out on the

highway, everyone who lives in Chena has a responsibility to help maintain peace in the village."

Frowning, Amanda looked up from where she squatted in front of the open refrigerator. "Of course. That's called good citizenship." She stood and closed the refrigerator door with a sharp snap. "And speaking of law and order, didn't you say you left two keys on the counter?"

"I did."

She began removing packaged foods from the box. "Actually, there was only one."

Kin shook his head. "I left two. You probably lost the other one during your move. You'll find it when you get straightened out here."

"I suppose that's possible. At any rate, I do like to carry a spare in case I lose a key when I'm out."

A grim look shadowed his chiseled features as he removed some canned goods from the box and set them on the counter. "I hope you're aware that this is not a village where you can go out partying every night. The one bar is only open on Friday night and we have very strict tribal rules about liquor here. You'll have to learn to arrange your own entertainment during your short stint in Chena."

Now, why would he bring that up? The man could be such a boor! She fumed for a silent moment, then spoke with cool formality. "Thank you for carrying my groceries, Mr. Russell. It really wasn't necessary to put yourself out. And please don't lose any sleep over my social life. I'm sure I'm much more creative than you realize."

She turned away, effectively dismissing him, and placed canned goods inside a cupboard. After a few moments of loaded silence, she heard the front door close sharply and turned to see that he had taken her broad hint and left. Her shoulders drooped and she rested her forehead against the cupboard door.

Why was he so angry? Yesterday, she thought she had seen interest in his eyes when he looked at her. Yet, he was constantly trying to make Chena sound like a horrible place to live. It was obvious he loved his village, but wanted Amanda out of it. Why?

Later that evening, she was arranging some of her favorite books on the bookcase in the loft when there was a knock on the door. She rushed down to open it, and found Kincaid with an older, distinguished-looking Athabascan man. She motioned them inside and hurriedly closed the door against the bitter air. They shrugged out of heavy parkas, placing them over the back of a chair.

"Miss Roberts, this is Pete Smith, the school principal," Kin said. "He thought he should meet you."

Pete smiled and gripped Amanda's hand firmly. "We're grateful that you came to Chena on such short notice, Miss Roberts. The teacher you're replacing decided after the first snowfall that Chena was just too isolated and cold for him. We hoped he'd at least stay for the full school year, but he hit the road the night the first term ended. There was no talking him out of it."

Amanda prepared coffee as they talked, ignoring Kin's challenging gaze and directing her attention to her new boss. "I'm excited to be here. This is a real adventure for a city-bred woman like me." When Kin's features turned skeptical, she gave him a menacing look.

They sat in the living room with cups of hot coffee while Pete explained the unique school system in Chena. He did most of the talking, answering Amanda's steady stream of questions while Kin watched her with cynical speculation and quietly examined Hailey the Hippo.

She knew he was appraising her, calculating how long he thought she'd last in this wilderness. Ruefully, she wondered if other teachers had been frightened away by the remote and rugged outpost that was Chena, or if they had in fact been frightened away by Kincaid Russell.

"Is that all right with you, Miss Roberts?" Pete's question penetrated her thoughts and brought her up with an embarrassing start.

She flushed and caught a look of gratified amusement on Kin's face. "I'm sorry. I was thinking. What was your question?"

"I was wondering if I could show you around the school tomorrow so you can prepare to take over your class?"

Amanda responded enthusiastically to the suggestion and they arranged to meet at the school the next morning.

"You do know you're going to be teaching four different grades in one classroom." He looked at her for confirmation and she nodded. "Since bush children grow up in mixed-grade classrooms, they usually handle it better than the teachers, at first."

With a toss of her head, Amanda laughed. "I'll probably be much more confused than they are."

Was that a look of approval in Kin's eyes? Sorely tempted to ask him what she had finally done right, she held her counsel due to Pete's presence. Then a mask dropped over Kin's weathered features, and he picked up the green hippo for further study. Had she just imagined that look because she wanted him to approve of her? Did he actually admire her eagerness to tackle a challenge, or was it wishful thinking?

It must be all in her mind, she decided. He was going to make her life in Chena harder than it had to be. As the self-appointed czar of Chena, he was set on doing just that.

While the principal made his way to the car, Kin turned to where Amanda stood in the doorway. "Who's your friend?" He nodded toward the hippo reclining on the couch.

Bracing for ridicule, Amanda looked down at her shoes before meeting his gaze with defiance. "Hailey the Hippo is somebody I saved all my money for when I was twelve. He's special, like teddy bears are to some people."

Those inscrutable eyes softened and he said in the gentlest voice she'd heard from him yet, "Tomorrow, you'll be receiving a load of firewood. It'll be stacked by the front door next to what's left. Keep a tarp over it to keep the snow off."

Surprised by his thoughtfulness, Amanda blinked. "Thank you."

As she watched in perplexity, he lifted a hand toward a strand of hair near her eyes, then stopped. She tentatively tucked the errant curl behind her ear, and he lowered his hand in the electrically charged silence.

He released a ragged breath, muttered a curt good

night, and went to join Pete in the Blazer. Long after they drove away, Amanda stood in the open door, watching the starry sky, unconscious of the cold.

Late that night she was reading in bed when a low droning sound from outside caused her to go downstairs to look out the window. She turned on a light and parted the curtains, casting a warm glow across the snow, to see what was happening on the airstrip. There was just enough moonlight to allow her to see a small plane taxiing without lights near the darkened lodge.

Two darkly clad figures soon emerged from the plane. They were joined by a third man getting out of an old canopied pickup truck sitting next to the runway. Uneasiness tickled Amanda's mind as they quickly began unloading boxes from the plane and placing them in the back of the truck. The general store was closed. Why would anyone be bringing supplies in now? With a shrug, Amanda turned away from the window. It was hardly her concern what time people chose to work.

Chapter Three

The morning was dark and the temperature far below zero. Amanda attempted to start the car, but it
only made weak gasping sounds before lapsing into
silence when she turned the key in the ignition. Repeated tries yielded no results, though there was gas
in the tank and she had never had trouble before.

As she crossed the slippery street to ask for help at
the lodge, Kincaid Russell's Blazer pulled up next to
her car. She ran haphazardly back toward him when
he went to open the tailgate.

"Mr. Russell!"

Suddenly, she slipped on a patch of ice and bar-
reled into him. They went down in a tangle of boots,
mittens, and scarves.

Kin offered a wry grin beneath Amanda's sprawled
form. "Well, you're certainly getting friendlier." His
face was mere inches from hers as he went on, his

hot breath fanning her flushed cheeks while his hands held her heavily clad figure. ''This is a welcome diversion, but I think we'd be a lot more comfortable inside, in front of a roaring fire.''

With a gasp of humiliation, Amanda pushed at his chest and struggled to move away from him on the ice. She was thankful for the darkness that concealed her heated flush. ''The ice . . . you don't think I—''

''I'd like to.'' Standing, he interrupted her weak stammer with a wicked smile. He reached down to help her up, and soon succeeded in forcing her to remain upright, despite her determination to succumb to the call of gravity and the ice.

They brushed snow from their clothing. ''Did I hurt you?'' she asked.

He spared her an appreciative glance. ''You're too small to do much damage. Physically, at least. You need to learn how to walk on ice, though. And why were you running away from the lodge?''

''I was going to ask for help at the lodge and then you drove up. I thought you might be able to help me start my car. I need to meet Mr. Smith at the school in a little while.''

''Well, let's see what ails the poor sucker.'' He walked around the car and lifted the hood. A quick glance was all he needed. ''You don't have a headbolt heater,'' he accused.

Amanda rolled her eyes. ''The heater works very well when the car is working,'' she said in a tone she would use for a child. ''I'd prove it if I could start the car.''

Kin moved around to open the driver's door and sit in the front seat. ''A headbolt heater is not the heater that keeps you warm, Princess,'' he explained in a patient voice. ''It's a heater that keeps the oil warm.''

He turned the key in the ignition several times but the car didn't make a sound. ''It's hopeless. You need to have a headbolt heater installed today. Then you plug it into an outdoor outlet. You flick on the switch inside the house to make the current run. It enables your car to start when you want it to, despite the cold.'' He shook his head ruefully. ''You'll never get this car running without it in our winter weather. Too cold.''

''I see,'' she said blankly, not seeing at all. Was he telling her she had to plug her car into the house to keep it operable? Surely she had misunderstood him. ''So where do I get this heater and the plugs and switches and things?'' *And how on earth do I figure out what to do with them when I get them?*

''All you need is the heater. Everything else is built into the house. It's electricity. I can have someone come and install the heater in the car for you today. How did you get through the Yukon in January without learning all this?''

She shrugged. ''Dumb luck?''

To solve the immediate problem, Kin offered to drive her to school. They unloaded her supplies from the station wagon and put them in the back seat of the Blazer. Amanda noticed the back of the vehicle was loaded with firewood.

Kin saw her eyeing the pile doubtfully. ''You'll be surprised at how much firewood you'll use.''

Upon their arrival at the school, he carried her supplies into Pete Smith's office. The principal motioned

Amanda to a chair and turned to Kin. " 'Morning, Kin. I didn't expect to see you today. Don't have enough to keep you busy?''

Kin laughed as he set Amanda's things on a corner of the principal's desk. ''Amanda's car wouldn't start, since she never heard of a headbolt heater. I'll be sure she gets one installed.'' He turned to her as she re- moved her scarf and mittens. ''Meantime, I'll call later to find out when you need a ride home.''

''I'll take her home, Kin. Don't worry about that.''

She quashed a sudden urge to tell Pete to mind his own business. For a brief moment, her heart had soared at the thought of seeing Kincaid Russell again in a few hours. Despite his prickly personality, there was something about him she liked. He always helped her even though he'd made it clear he felt she should leave. Elly's comment about his having been hurt by another woman from the Lower Forty-eight probably explained some of his harshness with her. Actually, that made it even more surprising that he still tried to help her, considering how he felt about cheechako women now. The way he looked at her made her feel very feminine and attractive. Unfortunately, he took Pete at his word and waved good-bye as he left the principal's office.

The principal showed Amanda around the school, explaining what grades were taught in each class. He appeared proud of the new gymnasium that had been added on to the back of the log school and pointed to the outdoor playground. The latter, he explained, was rarely used at this time of year, due to the ex- treme cold.

''The younger children spend recess and other recreational time in the gym during severe weather,'' he told her. ''Before the gym was added, we held recess in the hall and classrooms.''

Around noon, an attractive Athabascan woman entered the room as Amanda coordinated lesson plans for her four different groups of students. Thick, glossy black hair flowed in lustrous waves to the middle of her slender back and clear copper skin was accentuated by black wool slacks and a red cashmere sweater.

High heels clicked a light staccato on the tile floor as she moved gracefully to Amanda's desk with a warm smile. ''I'm Lucinda Smith. I teach fourth, fifth, and sixth grades. Daddy told me you were here to get settled before school reopens on Monday.''

Amanda shook the well-manicured hand proffered by the other woman, and thought she had never seen such exotic beauty. ''It's nice to meet a fellow teacher before school reopens. Mr. Smith didn't mention that his daughter was one of the teachers.''

''Yes, well, Daddy tries to keep our relationship out of the school completely,'' Lucinda said with a flutter of her crimson fingernails. ''He mentioned that Kin brought you in because your car was dead. I know things here are different for you and want to help you adjust in any way I can. I hope Kin wasn't too difficult. He can be very hard on cheechakos.''

She looked down at Amanda's work and nodded in satisfaction. ''Looks like you have things well under control.'' Pushing her hair over one shoulder, she bestowed another glittering smile upon Amanda. ''Well, I'd better get going. I'm off to Tok to do some shopping. Don't be afraid to call on me for anything.''

Amanda gazed after the woman in amazement as

she exited the room. What a whirlwind! Surely she was going to change into boots before going shopping. Wriggling her toes inside the wool socks and hiking boots encasing them, Amanda decided Lucinda might be strikingly beautiful, but she'd rather have warm feet.

Alone again, Amanda found it more difficult to concentrate on her work. A serious, weather-beaten copper face with liquid black eyes, framed by neatly cut straight black hair, kept floating above the papers on her desk. With a sigh, she attributed the pang in her stomach to hunger.

It was only two o'clock but already growing dark when Pete dropped Amanda at her house. Firewood was stacked neatly by the front door and, glancing at her frost-covered car, she noticed an electrical cord running from under the hood to an outlet on the wall of the house. Curious, she went to the car and, after several attempts, was able to start it.

So, the magic touch of Kincaid Russell had once again done the trick. A disgruntled feeling overtook her. He always seemed to know what he was talking about. Wasn't he ever wrong? She turned off the ignition and went into the chilly house.

After starting a fire in the Franklin stove, she decided the rest of her unpacking could wait until she'd had a decent meal. Nibbling on potato chips, she gathered together the things needed to prepare spaghetti and a tossed salad.

As she chopped an onion to add to the browning meat and garlic, Kin stopped by. His open smile faded instantly when she greeted him with a sniffle and wiped at red, running eyes with the back of her hand.

"What's wrong? Why are you crying?" He stepped inside and looked around for the cause of her tears.

With another sniffle, she chuckled. "I'm chopping an onion. I'm glad you're here. I want to thank you for your help today. I really appreciate the wood, the ride, and your work on my car. I guess things are a little different here in the bush than I expected." She waited for the gleeful "I told you so," but none came.

He gave a curt nod and led her to a switch on the dining room wall. "I wanted to show you the switch for turning the current to your headbolt heater on and off."

Amanda wished he'd kept his mundane reason for visiting to himself, but she planted a brittle smile on her face and listened dutifully to his simple instructions. An uncomfortable silence fell between them when he finished, and she cleared her throat awkwardly. "Uh, would you like to stay for an early dinner?"

Kin grazed a thumb down her cheek to remove an errant tear and his lips formed a tender smile. "Only on the condition that *I* finish chopping the onion."

Supressing a pleasant shudder at his gentle touch, she turned quickly toward the kitchen. They worked side by side while Kin regaled her with tales of moose and bear encounters in the bush. Many times, she was sure his tales were too tall to be believed, but she detected a deadly seriousness about the caution that was necessary when living among the wildlife.

"You've always got to remember where you are," he told her. "Even when couples go for romantic evening strolls in the summer, at least one of them carries a rifle.''

She envisioned starry-eyed couples juggling hearts and flowers and guns. ''Sounds charming,'' she said dryly before adding, ''Oh, I met Mr. Smith's daughter, Lucinda, today.''

Kin clumsily chopped tomatoes for a salad and replied absently, ''Lucy? We grew up together.''

Amanda was mildly surprised. ''She grew up in Chena? She seems so polished.'' Not wanting him to think she considered the villagers oafish, she rushed on. ''I mean, she seems like she'd be more at home in a Lower Forty-eight city than in a bush village,'' she explained, proud of her use of Alaskan terminology.

''Lucy should have stayed in the Lower Forty-eight after finishing college. She's never been very happy since she returned to Chena after living Outside. I don't know why she stays. She's never felt an especially strong tie to the tribe. She's . . .'' He hesitated and shrugged, before saying, ''Different.''

Turning down the heat under the spaghetti, Amanda nodded. ''Maybe she isn't sure what she wants to do. Although she certainly seems like a decisive person. Still, this is her home.''

His speculative eyes swept over her face. ''Feeling a little longing for your own home?''

''Not at all. Just trying to be empathetic. You should try it sometime.''

Kin grimaced in good humor. ''Ouch.''

''Yeah, well, you deserved it.''

He shrugged. ''Possibly. But I also know what I'm talking about—''

"I know, I know, as relates to life in the bush," she mimicked, before changing the subject. "Let's eat." Carrying the bowl of salad and a basket of garlic bread to the table, she motioned him to a chair.

Seating himself, Kin watched as she served up heaping plates of aromatic spaghetti. "You know, spunk is a good thing."

She regarded him through narrowed eyes. "But?"

"But it's no good without common sense."

Spaghetti sauce spattered his placemat as she set a plate in front of him none too gently. "Better eat before it gets cold," she said shortly.

The meal passed with both of them straining to avoid the subject foremost on their minds, that of his disapproval of her presence in Chena. They discussed neutral topics, from the weather to their favorite books and movies. Kin excused himself as quickly as was politely possible after dinner, saying he had to visit a friend.

Amanda bid him a stilted good night at the door and sighed in relief as he drove away. What had begun as a relaxed afternoon together had turned into a time thick with tension. Once again, he had managed to insult her. Why did she even put up with him?

After cleaning up the kitchen and putting away the dishes, Amanda returned to unpacking and organizing her new home. Throughout her work, she thought about Kin's strange mixture of rudeness and kindness toward her. At one turn, he tried to chase her out of town and at the other, he helped with her comfort in every way he could. He was absolutely the most frustrating man she had ever met. Too bad he was also the most handsome.

She slammed the linen closet door in vexation. Why was she so drawn to Kin, despite his determination to believe she was a hopeless city slicker? The pressure to succeed in the bush was stronger than ever.

It was a shame he was her landlord, because that would force her to deal with him on occasion. Still, she could try to avoid him as much as possible, and continue to formally call him by his last name to keep an emotional distance. Maybe once she was settled into the way of life in Chena, they wouldn't have to see so much of each other. Somehow, that thought didn't cheer her the way she expected.

In the earliest hours of the morning, she was awakened by a persistent scratching and whining downstairs at the front door. When the whines became howls and yips, she dragged herself out of bed and bundled into a fleecy robe and slippers. She turned on lights as she went down the stairs to the window near the door. Flicking on the porch light, she looked out into the dark, clear night and saw an emaciated pile of what could only be called orange fur huddled against the door. The animal scratched, whined, and shivered convulsively in the bitter cold.

When she opened the door, her heart went out to the small, freezing dog. His dark eyes, dull with cold and hunger, gazed up at her with a glimmer of hope. A bitter wind whistled into the house, causing Amanda to shiver almost as violently as the dog. Pure misery apparently overcame any fear he might feel as he allowed himself to be coaxed into the house. Quickly shutting the door, she led him to the wood-burning stove, where some warmth still emanated from the hot logs and ashes.

Getting an old blanket from the spare bedroom, Amanda covered his quaking form. The frost-covered animal huddled, shivering in front of the hearth, his bleary eyes following her every move.

She patted his head. "You poor little thing," she crooned as she rubbed warmth into him with the blanket. "I don't have any dog food, frosty fellow. But how about some spaghetti?"

Going to the kitchen, she spooned a portion of cold spaghetti onto a dish and placed it with a bowl of water on the floor in front of him. He sniffed cautiously before hungrily devouring the food. Aware that he was starving and would eat until he made himself sick if he could, she steeled herself against his pleading eyes when he'd finished his meal.

A lifelong love of animals poured itself into her movements as she comforted the dog. "More food in a few hours. Right now, you just warm up and go to sleep. That's what I'm going to do." Yawning widely, she turned out the lights and headed back up the stairs to bed.

Awakening a few hours later, she groped sleepily for the bedside lamp in the winter-morning darkness. When a flood of light bathed the room, she found the dog curled up next to her on the bed. He opened one eye and watched her, his scraggly tail thumping twice in pleasure when she reached over to stroke his stiff fur.

"You need a bath. But you'll get a reprieve for now."

Dressing in jeans and a blue angora sweater,

Amanda noticed the dog's adoring eyes watching her as she applied a touch of mascara, blush, and lipstick. He gave her an injured look when she ordered him off the bed so she could straighten the covers.

As she started down to the kitchen, she called, "How about some scrambled eggs, Frosty?" Though the dog immediately joined her, she was unsure if he was responding to his new name or hoping she would lead him to food. She suspected the latter.

She prepared scrambled eggs and toast, feeding Frosty with a portion of her own meal. Did his face actually fall when she promised him a dinner of regular dog food?

Hanging pictures on the walls and piling up the empty boxes was the order of the morning. In the afternoon, she walked to the general store to purchase a supply of canned dog food and was once again at the checkout counter when Kin entered the store, stomping snow from his boots.

Helping Van fill a cardboard box with the cans, Amanda ignored Kin's unsettling gaze. That constant disapproval was wearing pretty thin, and she'd just as soon he left her alone. Therefore, when he reached for the box, she held up a hand to stop him, saying firmly, "I can manage, thank you, Mr. Russell."

Kin's dark eyebrows rose in surprise and he stepped back to allow her to leave. "By all means."

Lifting the heavy box from the counter, Amanda gasped audibly. She struggled with the door, silently cursing Kin for coming in when he did. Out of the corner of her eye, she saw him standing where she had left him, arms casually folded across his chest, watching her while his mouth quirked in an obvious attempt to hold back laughter.

The door closed behind her and, too soon, she breathed a sigh of relief. She stepped down off the porch and onto a patch of ice hidden from view by the bulky box she carried. Her booted feet flew out from under her and the box went flying into the air, causing cans of dog food to roll all over the store yard. Amanda groaned loudly at the beating her tailbone took as she landed with a thud on the solid, icy ground.

A mirthful masculine voice spoke behind her. "You still haven't learned to walk on ice, I see."

Amanda turned on her derriere to look up into Kin's weather-beaten face, inwardly cringing at the laughter in his dark eyes. Ignoring the gloved hand he held out to her, she slid every which way on the ice, collecting cans and throwing them into the empty box that had landed nearby. Kin knelt and picked up one of the cans, reading the label.

His black eyes danced mischievously. "Tired of spaghetti, Princess?"

Amanda didn't deign to give him an answer, but grabbed the can from him and threw it in the box.

Kin tossed the remaining cans into the box and unceremoniously pulled Amanda to her feet. One strong gloved hand held her firmly under each arm.

Chest heaving, Amanda pushed against both him and the whirling sensations his touch brought to life inside her. Humiliation at having fallen on the ice in front of him twice in as many days convinced an irrational part of her that he must be to blame. "Let me go."

He ignored her protest, his breath warm on her face. ''Press your toes and the balls of your feet firmly to the ground.''

The temptation to refuse was strong. Still, Amanda suspected that if she did, he would let go of her. In consideration of her sore tailbone, she decided it would be prudent to swallow her bruised pride and do as he instructed. Any remaining shreds of dignity demanded that she remain upright on the slick ground. So, doing as he instructed, she tried again to push away from him.

He continued to grip her with firm hands. His eyes lingered on her lips, mere inches from his own. ''That is how you stand and walk on ice. It's not foolproof, but you won't find yourself constantly flying through the air, either.''

''Thank you. You can let me go now.''

Kin slowly removed his hands from her and picked up the box of dog food. When Amanda reached to take it from him, he gave her an exasperated look and walked purposefully down the street toward the A-frame. Amanda hurried to catch up with him and the short walk was again made in silence. They were greeted at the door by a wriggling mass of bones and fur.

Kin set the box on the kitchen counter and bent to fondle the animal's ears. ''I didn't know you had a dog.''

Uh-oh. Nervous fingers fumbled with the zipper of her coat. ''I didn't until last night. He was freezing and starving and we sort of adopted each other.'' *Please don't make me get rid of him. I couldn't do it.* She took off her coat and tossed it on a chair. ''Thank you for helping me with the box,'' she added grudgingly.

Kin smiled, his white teeth a flash of lightning in his dark face. He swept off his fur hat and executed a flourishing bow. ''Always glad to help a lady in distress.''

That dashing smile caused her heart to flutter, and she removed the cans from the box to distract herself. ''I hope you don't mind my having Frosty here,'' she said with a glance at the dog.

He looked dubious as his eyes followed hers to the fluorescent mutt busily sniffing his mukluks. ''Frosty? His name is Frosty?''

Amanda felt a need to defend the unlikely name she had given her new pet. ''Well, he was so cold and frosty when I found him, the name just sort of stuck.'' She opened one of the cans and scooped the contents into a bowl.

Kin watched the starving animal lunge at the food Amanda set on the kitchen floor. ''Oh. Well, I don't have any problem with him. I love dogs. Have one or two of my own, in fact.''

Amanda pulled a carton of milk out of the refrigerator and poured some into a pan. ''I don't suppose you have time for a cup of cocoa. I hear you're the busiest man in town.'' Knowing how he disapproved of her, it went against the grain to make the offer, but it was the only polite thing to do after he had helped her with the heavy box. With some trepidation and a distinct feeling of exhilaration, she watched him shrug out of his parka.

Noting her wide-eyed regard, his mouth twitched with amusement. Of course, she hadn't expected him to accept the offer. ''Never too busy for cocoa or kisses.''

The pan of milk landed on the stove with a bang, almost slipping from her hand at his words. Blood began to pound in her temples and the breath caught in her throat when she saw his eyes dance as he eased his long legs over a bar stool at the open counter. The man knew just how to fluster her and took great joy in that knowledge!

''So, tell me. Besides a consuming need for adventure, and earning a livelihood, what brings you to Chena?''

Happy to be distracted from his disturbing gaze, Amanda crossed her arms and leaned against the refrigerator, a thoughtful frown creasing her forehead. ''I grew up pretty sheltered. Halfway through college at a private women's school, I realized I knew nothing about the so-called 'real world.' For a change of routine, I took classes in Native American studies. Thought it would be good to learn about the other basic American culture.'' She hesitated at the skepticism that lurked in his eyes.

''And those classes qualify you to teach the Indians in Chena?''

His attitude irked her and she felt her nerves tighten. ''My education and teaching experience qualify me to teach anywhere. I emphasized that when this job opening came up. Indians are people, Mr. Russell. They deserve an education and have hopes and dreams just like anyone else. I don't believe they want to be treated like strange beings with strange needs. I believe they want to be treated with simple respect, like people everywhere.'' She recognized a look of grudging respect in his eyes.

''Why didn't you transfer to a large coed university, or travel, when you needed to learn more about the world?''

''My parents wanted me tucked safely away at that little women's college in a small town. I needed to finish my formal education and they were footing the bill.''

''Can't argue with that logic.'' He watched her move restlessly around the kitchen. ''So, you're here to prove something to the world.''

Amanda took two heavy mugs from a cupboard and set them on the counter. Swallowing hard, she lifted her chin, and met his gaze head-on. ''I have nothing to prove, Mr. Russell.'' She thought of her father and his insistence that she would never survive on her own out here. Kin had the same low opinion of her. *They're both wrong. I have nothing to prove to anyone but myself. I'll do fine out here if certain men will just stop treating me like some delicate, mindless female.*

Kin's eyes narrowed at the visible whirl of emotions crossing Amanda's face. His dubious look made it plain he didn't believe her bold statement, that he was convinced she wanted to prove something.

Amanda bit her lip and turned quickly back to the stove to rescue the hot milk. Her erratic pulse caused her hand to shake as she mixed cocoa in with the milk. Why did this man have such a devastating effect on her senses? She was always falling or dropping things when he was around. No wonder he thought she didn't belong in the bush.

A change of subject was necessary if she was going to draw his attention away from herself and regain some semblance of control over the situation. With the pan of cocoa in hand, she turned to him. "Are there any Indian reservations around here?"

The twinkle in his eyes told her he hadn't missed her strategic attempt to move out of the spotlight. "There are none in Alaska," he said, watching her pour steaming cocoa into the mugs.

She put two fluffy white marshmallows in each mug. "I understand you have a head chief."

Kin's eyes searched her face for a moment. "He's not a head chief, he's *the* Chief. Chief Chena. He's the man who settled Chena. The tribe used to be nomadic before he settled it here prior to World War II. His son will eventually become chief. We don't have elections here. It's passed on in families."

She gave him an impish grin. "I thought *you* ran this town."

"I do."

The reassertion of that familiar arrogance caused her to feel a flicker of irritation. Carrying mugs of creamy cocoa, she walked past him to the couch. Another change of subject seemed in order before he could annoy her any further.

She faced him and held out one of the mugs. "Here's your cocoa, but I'm afraid I'm *fresh* out of kisses," she said lightly, knowing he was astute enough to recognize she was labeling him "fresh."

With a grin and a slight bow of his head, Kin acknowledged the hit.

Amanda seated herself on the couch. "I've noticed the airfield is pretty busy here. And I saw the FAA tower,'' she commented. She felt pleased with herself for being able to discuss activities in the community so soon after her arrival.

Joining her, he accepted the cup of cocoa. ''The field is busy, but the tower is only open during regular government hours. No swing or midnight shifts for those guys.''

Amanda sipped a bit of cocoa around the marshmallows bobbing on the surface. ''What about emergency landings?''

''You've seen enough of Chena to know we have no facilities to handle any kind of emergency, and the FAA is very strict about landings here, mainly because of our proximity to the border.'' Kin tasted his own cocoa and smiled in approval. ''Planes can't land here at night because the tower is closed. Tok is the closest place for emergencies.''

''I've seen a plane land here at night,'' she said airily.

The look he shot her was condescending. ''What you've seen is a plane landing during the dark hours of a typical northern winter day. Remember, it's dark during most of the day here in winter.''

Amanda felt her hackles rise. As if she didn't know the difference between day and night. ''I've seen a plane land at night, Mr. Russell. I know the difference between day and night, even when it's dark. I happen to own a clock or two.'' She took another sip of cocoa and then made a great show of counting on her fingers. ''Let's see . . . by my calculations, twelve-thirty in the morning is considered night hours by the FAA.''

Kin sat up straight and put his mug on the varnished birch coffee table. His mercurial eyes sharpened as he turned his gaze fully on Amanda. "You saw a plane land after midnight?"

Eagerly, she rushed to reassure him. "Yup. But it was just a quiet little one. It didn't cause any disturbance at all. I probably wouldn't even have heard it if I'd been asleep when it came in. I was reading and peeked out when I heard the noise."

He leaned forward and spoke in a controlled voice. "Well, now that you know the sound, don't bother peeking anymore. Just ignore it."

"Maybe I will. Maybe I won't." She was aware she sounded like a child, but this man had the most maddening way of giving orders and expecting everyone to follow them. Someone had to take him down a peg. Since everyone else in town worshipped him, she figured it was up to her to do just that.

"Amanda, it's none of your concern what goes on at that airfield. Planes shouldn't be landing here at that hour. Ignore it next time, okay?"

"Don't try to dictate my every move just because you're my landlord. You may run this village, but you don't run me. I'll do as I please, within the limits of the law. Besides, it's probably just some hunters coming home or something." She shook her head in bewilderment. "Why are we even talking about this? This is a stupid thing to argue about."

His jaw clenched. "It's in your best interest to take my advice on matters pertaining to Chena. You don't know anything about this village or its concerns."

"I guess I'll just have to learn about them now that I'm a resident."

"I'm warning you for your own good."

''Warning me? About what?''

Kin's eyes slid evasively away from hers and he waved a careless hand. ''I'm just concerned about you.''

''Well, I've had enough of your concern the past couple of days to last me a lifetime.''

His tone became harsh as he stood and went to pick up his parka and gloves, pulling them on with vicious, jerky movements. ''Just remember what I told you. Don't watch planes in the middle of the night here. They shouldn't be landing, so you're watching something you obviously shouldn't know about. You're better off ignoring it.'' His face was grim as he went out the door, a speechless Amanda at his heels, bristling with indignation as she closed the door forcefully behind him.

Cleaning up the cocoa things, she fumed at his high-handedness. A tiny corner of her mind told her she was overreacting again. But if she had overreacted to his orders, he had certainly overdramatized her watching of night planes. Where was the harm in that activity?

What really bothered her was the disappointment she felt at his abrupt departure. Sternly, she reminded herself that only yesterday she had decided not to get too friendly with him. He was on a serious power trip. Definitely a man to steer clear of.

There had to be some other explanation for the way her pulse raced and her nerves quivered when he was near. Maybe it was the change of climate. Her body must be trying to adjust itself to the extreme cold. She couldn't allow herself to believe for one minute that she was actually interested in such an impossible man. It had to be the weather.

A familiar, low droning sound around eleven o'clock that night caused her to lay aside one of the three mystery novels she was currently engrossed in. The thought of Kin made her march triumphantly to the window and, parting the curtains, she looked with careless abandon at the plane. Once more, it landed without lights, and she wondered if it was the same one.

While she watched with new awareness, Kin's dire warning echoed through her mind. Could there actually be something shady going on out there? Why was he so adamant about keeping her ignorant about the reason for his warning? Obviously, he suspected something, or—and this thought frightened her more than she wanted to admit—he was personally involved in something questionable and didn't want her snooping. Doggedly, she continued her surveillance.

There was a pickup truck on the airfield to meet the plane, just like before. Three men unloaded boxes from the plane and placed them in the back of the pickup. When the loaded truck headed for the edge of the field to join the narrow road running past her house, Amanda felt increasingly nervous. Just as the truck was about to pass her house, she turned away from the window.

Hers was the only house in town that overlooked the airfield. It was possible, she supposed as she headed back upstairs, that nobody else knew about the late-night landings. But it was awfully hard to believe anything crooked could be going on in this little burg.

However, she was still unable to resist the urge to look out the upstairs window, and saw the plane take off into the night sky without any lights as the truck left the airfield and slowly passed her house. Looking down through the window, she was disconcerted and a little unnerved to see the grim countenance of a bearded man watching her. Her eyes seemed to lock with his and she shivered involuntarily when he continued to look back and up at her as the truck moved on.

One hand went to her throat, where her heart thumped wildly, and she turned sharply away from the bedroom window. Surely, her imagination was just working overtime because she was reading three mysteries at once. That would explain what had felt like a menacing look coming from the face in the truck window. After all, she was just a harmless schoolteacher, interested in the activities of the village. Nobody had any reason to be bothered by her curiosity.

But if that's true, why is Kincaid Russell so upset about my nocturnal spying? her inner voice asked ominously.

Chapter Four

The next morning, Amanda dressed in a plaid wool skirt and moss-green silk blouse for her first day of teaching. She pulled on knee-high black leather boots with heels and a camel cardigan before bundling into her coat and mittens. The morning air was subzero, but her car started without hesitation and she let it idle with the heater and defroster running full blast while she cautiously moved around it, scraping frost from the windows.

Arriving early at the school so she could ensure everything was ready for her students, she encountered Pete Smith in the hall. He glanced at her stylish boots and then held her arm as they walked to the classroom. Amanda was grateful for his support when she slipped twice as the snow from her boots melted on the smooth tile floor.

"Miss Roberts, I believe you'd find a pair of mukluks not only safer but warmer in this climate," he suggested. "I'm sure you've seen them on people since you arrived in Chena. They're a type of boot made of caribou hide and trimmed with seal fur and beadwork. They're created by the Eskimo and the sole won't slip as easily as the type of boots you have on now."

She placed an armful of books and papers on her desk. "I've seen Mr. Russell in them. I haven't noticed any in the general store, though."

"No. You'd have to go to Tok for them. Have you been there yet?"

"I've been too busy adjusting to my new surroundings. I might go on Saturday." She moved to the teacher's closet in a corner of the classroom.

"I'm glad to see Kin was successful in getting your car running again," her boss said.

"Yes, Mr. Russell has been very . . . helpful." Amanda removed her coat.

"Helpful is my middle name," claimed a familiar masculine voice from the doorway. Kincaid Russell, bundled in his fur parka, his face framed by the fur-ruffed hood, sauntered into the room. " 'Morning, Pete. Just wanted to make sure our cheechako arrived safely for her first day with the kids."

" 'Morning, Kin. Well, I'd better get back to the office. Just call on the intercom if you need anything, Miss Roberts," Pete said as he left the room.

Left alone with Kin, Amanda determinedly attributed her sudden shivers to the removal of her heavy coat. A low whistle from Kin caused her to spin around and find his admiring gaze on her. She could feel the heat rising in her cheeks.

His eyes were dark and appreciative. "You look sharp for a resident of Chena."

Hanging her coat in the closet, Amanda wondered if this was yet another way of telling her she didn't fit in, but replied, "Thank you. Lucinda also dresses sharply for a resident of Chena, don't you think?"

"I haven't seen Lucinda this morning so I can't give her the same compliment."

Amanda closed the closet door with a snap and headed for her desk. Picking up a pile of textbooks, she studiously avoided meeting his eyes in hopes he would feel properly chastised for trying to give her orders yesterday.

He watched her place the various textbooks for different grade levels on the desks she had previously arranged in separate groupings. "Looking forward to meeting the kids?" His query broke the silence that threatened to lengthen between them and he walked to where Amanda was gathering another pile of books.

"Yes."

With a slight frown, he looked at her curiously. "What's the matter, Princess?"

Amanda's movement away from him was arrested when he grabbed her with strong hands. An armful of books remained between them as he pulled her against him, and her skin burned where his hands gripped her arms. He pushed a strand of hair away from her face, his thumb running down her cheek, leaving a fiery trail of sensation.

His gaze was warm, his eyes intent on her face. She should pull away before she became hopelessly lost in the deep pools of his eyes. His thumb on her cheek left a trail of fire and her tongue traced lips grown dry from the harsh climate. Kin's eyes told her he hadn't missed the gesture. He was going to kiss her, and she wanted him to. Oh, how she wanted him to.

His dark features blurred as his face descended toward hers, stopping at a sound from the doorway behind him. He turned abruptly away and they faced the crooked grin of a dark-haired teenage boy.

Amanda moved quickly across the room to place the books on the groupings of freshman desks. Guilt assailed her at the knowledge that she had wanted Kin to kiss her, *still* wanted it in fact. Students would be pouring in soon, and she was willing to throw discretion to the wind. Good grief! This was her first day on the job, in a new town, and a tiny one at that, where word spread like wildfire. *I must be out of my mind,* she mentally kicked herself as she felt a heated flush creep up her neck.

"Hi, Tom," Kin said as the boy sauntered into the room. "How's your sister's new baby?"

"Cool." Tom's eyes darted from Kin to Amanda and back again. "Noisy, though."

"Good lungs, huh?" Kin responded knowingly. He placed an arm around the youth's shoulders and turned to Amanda. "Mandy—er, Miss Roberts, this is Tom Dilling. He's in the eleventh grade."

Tom frowned. "I'm a junior, man."

Kin smiled winningly at Amanda with a look that said, *"And he's all yours."*

"It's nice to meet you, Tom." Amanda smiled and motioned to her desk. "Since you're here early, would you like to help me put books on the desks?"

He shrugged. "Sure. I know which books each grade uses." He went to pick up a stack of *Romeo and Juliet* paperbacks for the freshman desks. "*Romeo and Juliet*. How appropriate." He smirked. The dark look Kin shot him only made him laugh with relish and move across the room with great speed to distribute the books.

Covering embarrassment with formality, Amanda turned to Kin and held out her hand. "Thank you for your assistance, Mr. Russell. Have a nice day."

Kin took her hand in his and softly stroked her palm with his rough thumb. "Any time at all, Miss Roberts. I'll be seeing you soon." Giving her hand a gentle squeeze, he turned and left the room.

Taking a deep breath to steady her erratic pulse, Amanda reached for another stack of books. With Tom in the room, she forced herself to act nonchalant, even though her knees wanted to give way beneath her.

The week went by smoothly and on Friday she congratulated herself at how well things were going with her students. She'd not seen Kin since Monday and had heard through the Chena grapevine that he had gone to Anchorage on business. It should have been a relief not having him around to criticize or make her uncomfortable, but an empty feeling rocked her heart whenever she thought of him.

On Friday evening she decided to treat herself to dinner at the lodge. She settled into a booth looking out over the dark airfield and began a list of items to shop for in Tok the next day while waiting for Elly to take her order.

"That Lucinda," the Native American woman said breathlessly, shuffling out of the kitchen and over to Amanda's table. "I swear, that girl needs to move to the city. She wants me to get in touch with Kin about doing some citified shopping she wants done. He's already on his way back, though." She sighed gustily. "She just don't got no business here, no more."

"It *is* rather surprising that she stays," Amanda conceded. "I'd think she'd like city life."

Elly waved her order pad wildly. "She loves it. Went to college in a city, you know. Guess she stays 'cause of Kin. On again, off again, you know." She poised a pen over her tablet and eyed Amanda. "Now, what can I get you?"

For a moment, the words caught in Amanda's throat. Why would Lucinda stay because of Kin? Did Kin and Lucinda have a relationship? *Well, so what if they do? It means nothing to me. Right?* She realized Elly was watching her expectantly and murmured something about the fried chicken dinner.

Questions about Kin and Lucinda buzzed through Amanda's mind while she ate. She had pushed her plate to one side and was gazing blindly out the window, deep in thought about the possibilities, when Paul Donaldson joined her. After Elly took his order, they talked desultorily about various things until Amanda glanced out at the empty airfield and remembered her argument with Kin about aircraft landing at night.

Until she knew if Kin was involved in something shady, it wouldn't do to tip off the police. She wasn't sure if she had really seen something she shouldn't, or if Kin was just acting high-handed again. During a lull in the conversation, she affected a casual tone. "Do a lot of planes land here?"

Paul's reply was delayed by Elly's arrival with his mooseburger and fries. She refilled both their coffee cups and shuffled back to the kitchen. Paul began eating and periodic pauses allowed him to tell Amanda about aircraft coming into Chena.

"Most of the planes landing here come from Canada. A Customs or Immigration officer drives out from the border to inspect them when the FAA calls. Alaskan planes sometimes stop here for refueling, too. Especially if they're headed into Canada, where fuel costs more."

He took a healthy bite out of his burger and looked out the window. It seemed an interminable time to Amanda before he chewed, swallowed, and continued.

"Most are small, private planes, but once in a while we get a Canadian military plane. Our strategic location in the bush, and near the border, makes it a busy field for such a tiny village."

At least Paul doesn't act cloak-and-daggerish about the planes, she noted to herself. "Do they land around the clock?"

Paul spread a liberal dose of ketchup on the remains of his mooseburger. "No. Only when the FAA is in the tower, which is during regular government hours, seven days a week."

Amanda thoughtfully nibbled on a cold french fry as she thought about Kin's attitude versus Paul's. She considered telling Paul about the planes she had seen landing at night, but hesitated at the thought that he, like Kin, might become unreasonably angry and not tell her why. Her curiosity increased as people kept telling her there were no night flights in or out of Chena. Kin probably just got angry because she had discovered something going on that he didn't already know about. After all, he said he ran the town, so he probably expected to be the first to know everything.

The planes were probably just locals coming home. So, they happened to arrive after the FAA was closed. So what? Surely the rules weren't so strict that local residents weren't allowed to come home whenever they pleased.

She had read somewhere that Alaska contained the largest number of private pilots per capita in the United States, because most of the state was unreachable, except by air. Hundreds of bush pilots flew hunters and fishermen out to the wilds, year-round, and a lot of locals had small planes. The boxes she had seen being unloaded from those late-night planes into the waiting pickup were probably full of hunter's bounty. Or were they?

Amanda's mental study was interrupted by a rush of cold air and the disquieting arrival of Kin as he entered the lodge, stomping snow from his mukluks. His dark gaze met hers across the room for a loaded moment and then moved to the lanky form of the trooper sitting across from her. Something flickered in his eyes before an unreadable mask dropped over his face and he moved toward the kitchen in silence.

Paul looked up in time to see Kin and stood quickly. "Back in a minute." With a vacant smile, he headed for the kitchen.

Amanda chewed her bottom lip and tried to turn her attention back to her shopping list. The deep dis-

cussion that ensued when Paul met Kin coming out
with a sandwich in his hand distracted her. Whatever
they were discussing appeared serious. Paul ques-
tioned Kin in low tones and listened intently to Kin's
responses.

Amanda nibbled on another cold fry and strained
her ears to hear what they were saying. She almost
choked when she saw Kin point in her direction while
explaining something to Paul and frown openly when
Paul glanced at her, still talking animatedly. Kin
scowled and shook his head and Amanda sighed in
exasperation and finished chewing. She was tempted
to walk over to them and demand to know what they
were saying. As she considered that course of action,
Kin suddenly lost patience with Paul and spoke
fiercely.

"No. She is to be told nothing. This is a tribal
matter and doesn't concern her. I don't want her involved." With those parting words, he stalked off
down the hall where his office and the guest rooms
were located.

Amanda seethed with curiosity as Paul rejoined
her, but decided questioning him would be to no avail
due to Kin's final words. She resented their talking
about her in her presence.

In hopes that a simple question tossed out to Paul
would glean some information, she gave him a dis-
arming smile. "What have I done to displease Mr.
Russell now?"

Paul's usually earnest blue eyes were guarded as
he looked at her. "What do you mean?"

Maybe he would let down his guard if she feigned
intense disinterest. "I mean he was talking about me

and was angry, as usual. What did he have to say?''
Oh, boy, that really sounds disinterested.

Paul's next words made it clear she wasn't going to worm any answers out of him concerning his conversation with Kin. "Oh, I guess he's just angry at the world right now. His trip to Anchorage must not have gone very well. Would you like more coffee?"

Not wanting to cause him further discomfort by persisting in her questioning, Amanda let the matter drop. Kincaid Russell could be a formidable adversary and Paul obviously did not take his instructions lightly. And why was Paul taking orders from Kin, anyway? Kin was a lot of things to this community, but Chief of Police he was not. It must be a personal matter between them. Still, none of that explained why they were discussing her.

"I realize it's a major decision."

She heard Paul's chuckle and looked blank. "What is?"

He gave her a broad smile. "Whether or not you want more coffee."

Her apologetic grin turned into a chuckle and then an outright laugh. Paul's laughter blended with hers, and they sounded like a couple of revelers when Kin returned to the dining room. He stopped at the sound of their mirth and, giving them a dark look, entered the kitchen. Shortly, they heard the slam of the door that led outside.

A firm knock on her door that evening interrupted Amanda just when she was coming to the climax of the latest "Mrs. Pollifax" spy mystery. Irritated, and with the book still in her hand, she warily invited Kin inside and took his parka. Why was he there when he hadn't even seen fit to give her the time of day at the lodge, after being out of town all week?

He glanced around. "Are you alone?"

"No. Frosty is here." Reluctantly placing her book on the kitchen counter, she turned on the heat under the teakettle.

The corners of his mouth turned up in amusement and he ruffled the clean fur of the dog, who padded into the kitchen at the sound of his name. "Looks like he had a bath."

Amanda grimaced. "The trauma of his life," she assured him.

Kin smiled and seated himself on a stool outside the counter. "How was your first week with the kids?"

"It went well. They're a good group. I just have to get used to teaching four grade levels in one class. It can get a little crazy sometimes."

Kin had grown up in mixed-grade classrooms and gave an understanding nod. "Have you been to Tok yet?"

"No. I'm going tomorrow." She reached into a cupboard and withdrew two mugs.

He nodded again and picked up her novel, reading the title. His gaze roamed around the house, coming to rest on two four-foot-long rows of paperback mysteries propped up with bookends on the living room coffee table. There was just enough space left on the table for coffee cups to be set if necessary. "You've made the place look mighty cozy," he admitted. "But aren't you a little short on reading material?"

"Yeah, I need to join the Book-of-the-Month club

or something, now that I live out here,'' she replied seriously, then saw his teasing grin and flushed at her own gullibility.

Fiddling with the handles of the mugs, she itched to know the reason for his unexpected visit. The last time they'd been together, he had been about to kiss her in the classroom. Her skin tingled at the memory and her palms felt moist as she imagined how it would have felt.

''I think it's hot.''

His words brought her sharply out of her reverie. How could he know? What was he, a mind reader? She stared at him, trying to comprehend how he knew what she had been thinking about. ''Uh . . .''

Kin pointed a finger at the stove. ''The water. In the kettle. I think it's hot.'' He watched her closely. ''You okay, Mandy?''

Thank you, she prayed silently. *He doesn't read minds after all, and my pride remains intact—for now, at least.* She removed the boiling kettle from the stove and filled the mugs with hot water. ''Tea or cocoa?'' She replaced the kettle on the stove and opened a cupboard.

''Cocoa.'' He smiled when Amanda handed Frosty a dog biscuit at the same time she removed a can of cocoa. ''Are you taking Frosty to the vet in Tok?''

''No. Just going because it's there.''

''You really should take him for some shots, Mandy. You don't know anything about a stray.'' He gave the wandering dog an affectionate pat. ''There are lots of wild animals around here. And most of the tame ones run loose.''

''Yeah, I've found that out.'' A direct, wise look

at him left her feeling gratified to see him uncharac-
teristically flustered.

"Well, he should be examined and vaccinated." A
dark flush deepened the color of his face as he attempted to keep the focus of the conversation on
Frosty.

There was wisdom in what he said and she considered his advice as they took the mugs and moved into
the living room. Mezmerized, she watched Kin's muscles cord when he placed another log on the low-
burning fire. He stoked it to a roaring blaze before
joining her on the couch.

"Maybe I'll take him with me and visit a vet," she
conceded. "Do you have any idea where he might
have come from?"

Kin shook his head. "Just another pup abandoned
by someone. Most of the pets around here aren't
spayed or neutered. There's not a lot of money for
things like that here."

A comfortable silence fell between them as they
sipped cocoa and watched the fire. Kin fingered
Hailey Hippo's tattered red ribbon and Amanda decided he was a very nice companion when he wasn't
trying to be disagreeable.

Setting Hailey aside, Kin shifted on the couch and
crossed a muklukked foot over his knee. "I hope
you're ready for a snowfall. The temperature has
risen. It's going to snow tonight and then it's bound
to freeze hard again."

"I've been hoping for some fresh snow. The old
stuff is looking pretty gray."

He watched her intently, something unfathomable

in the depths of his eyes. His next words were quiet. "Let me take you to Tok tomorrow."

She sat up straight, immediately on guard. "No," she stated flatly, with a vigorous shake of her head. "Absolutely not."

He acted as though she hadn't spoken. "We'll make a day of it," he enthused. "Frosty can go to the vet for a good checkup and some vitamins and shots and I'll squire you around Tok, small as it is. You may want to pick up a few things. Their groceries are a little less expensive than the ones in my store and—"

"No. I'm going alone."

His voice was soft as he put his foot back on the floor, squeezed his mug onto the cramped table in front of them, and edged closer to her. "Are you afraid of me, Princess?"

She moved away from him and felt the wide, cushioned arm of the couch behind her. "Don't be ridiculous," she sputtered with a little too much spirit.

Kin's gaze followed the play of emotions running across her face, and he stretched an arm behind her. His warm hand enveloped hers for a moment as he took her mug and set it beside his own.

When Amanda started to get up, his arm slid down around her shoulders. He reached with a weather-roughened hand to stroke her soft cheek, and his face was very close to hers as he ran a hand gently through her hair.

She turned her face away from his. "Kin—"

With a ghost of a smile, he said, "You know, that's the first time you've ever called me by my first name.

You really are getting friendlier. Even though I think you're trying very hard not to.''

''Kin, don't—'' She turned toward him, but he stifled any further words she might have to say by covering her mouth with his own.

His hands entwined in her tangled hair as he cuddled her close, and she was vaguely aware of the feel of his racing heartbeat before she felt his breath feather lightly across her cheek. There was such tenderness in his eyes before he kissed her again, sending her senses reeling. Her fingers clutched at his thick black hair and then crept slowly down the length of his back. Something deep in her consciousness screamed that she was setting herself up for serious heartache if she allowed herself to care too much for him.

''N-no. Don't.''

He closed his eyes with a sigh and lay his cheek against hers. ''Mandy, Mandy, what are you afraid of?''

A sharp rap sounded on the door just then, causing her to jump guiltily as strength returned to her body. She placed her hands on his chest to push him away.

Her guilty look caused him to grin lazily. ''Who are you afraid that is? Your mother?''

Her breath came in gasps and she pushed at his solid chest. ''I . . . uh . . . let go of me so I can go answer it,'' she whispered frantically.

He planted a kiss on her earlobe. ''Let's ignore it and practice more friendliness.''

She struggled again and fixed him with a stern look. ''We can't. The door isn't locked. If I don't answer it, they could come in on us.''

He moved away with reluctance, eyes twinkling as Amanda tried to smooth her hair into place. Her breathing was still uneven.

When she opened the door and Lucinda stepped over the threshold, bundled in a luxurious, thigh-length black fur parka, Amanda was speechless with shame. Then she caught the look of annoyance that crossed Kin's features and her heart gave a little leap.

"Hello," she said dumbly to the woman in front of her.

Lucinda's gaze took in Amanda's disheveled hair and flushed cheeks. "Hello, Amanda." She turned to Kin. "Kin, your grandfather has been waiting for you to get back from Anchorage all day. He needs to speak with you about something very important. Cliff, at the bar, said you were coming over here for something a while ago."

Annoyance written on his face, Kin rose from the couch while Amanda picked up his parka from a chair and handed it to him. "My Blazer is at the lodge. I'll drive to Grandfather's house from there."

Probably feeling guilty, like me, Amanda thought with a mental cringe.

With a smile for Amanda, Lucinda went out the door. Kin took Amanda's hand in both of his. "Thank you for the cocoa and . . . other things, Mandy. See you in the morning."

"No!"

He winked at her, pulled on his gloves, and headed out into the cold night. Snow had begun falling a short time earlier and the crunching sound of his mukluks on the old, crusty snow was muffled as he walked over to the lodge.

Amanda closed the door behind her and leaned against it, her senses spinning with the still-fresh feeling of his sweet kisses. No man had ever made her feel the way he did. With Kin, she felt as if she were falling into a bottomless and incredibly soft, warm pit lined with pillows and clouds. She feared the feeling was addicting and wondered how she could even consider falling for a man who disdained her very existence in his world.

Kin's refusal to believe in Amanda's ability and determination to carve out a life for herself in the bush was a major obstacle. She simply couldn't overlook that or allow herself to become seriously involved with a man who had no faith in her strength and fortitude. Men like that smothered and belittled women. She would die if she weren't allowed to explore and grow.

But, boy, what a way to go! Her face still tingled where his kisses had touched her sensitive skin. She sat on the couch, reliving every moment of the enchanted evening, seeing herself and Kin cuddling in the flames of the slowly dying fire.

It was late when she was roused from her meditation by a familiar low droning sound outside. Moving to the window, she looked out through the curtains to see a private plane land and taxi to a dark pickup waiting at the northeast edge of the airfield.

Tired after her busy week and the emotionally charged moments with Kin, she went to open the door and let Frosty out for a short run. The activity on the airfield ceased as light from her open doorway shone across the snow. They were probably just curious about the cheechako schoolteacher, she told herself in a nervous attempt to dismiss the uncomfortable feeling of being watched while she waited for the dog.

Once Frosty was safely back inside the warm house, Amanda prepared for bed. She turned out the bedside lamp and snuggled down under the warm blankets on the bed in the loft. Kin had acted like he was determined to take her to Tok tomorrow. Well, he might show up, but there was no way he could make her go with him!

Chapter Five

Darkness still blanketed the winter morning when Amanda was awakened by the sound of barking dogs. Tumbling out of bed, she pulled on her robe, her feet searching the carpeted floor for slippers, before she rushed down the stairs to the front window. When she parted the curtains, she thought she'd stepped backward in time into Edna Ferber's novel, *Ice Palace*.

A team of seven excited huskies, their thick coats intricately designed with marks of black on white, was harnessed to an authentic wooden dogsled outside her house. Methodically moving from one dog to another, talking and checking their restraints, was Kincaid Russell, bundled in his fur parka, mukluks, and thick fur mittens. The clock on the dining room wall told Amanda that it was only seven o'clock as she simultaneously flicked on a light and opened the door.

Seeing her shivering in the open doorway in her

robe and slippers, Kin straightened up from his one-way conversation with one of the huskies. With a gallant bow, he waved one arm at the dogsled. "Your chariot awaits, my lady." His eyes twinkled joyfully, daring her to refuse to go "mushing" with him.

"Are you crazy? It's seven o'clock on Saturday morning," she grumbled irritably as she tried to shake the sleep from her brain. "I must be dreaming. This can't be real."

His feet made no sound as he walked toward her across the soft, powdery snow that had fallen during the night. "I would suggest a slightly different mode of dress for our trip to Tok. And has anyone ever told you how beautiful you look in the morning?"

"Spreading it on a bit thick, aren't you, Mr. Russell? And I told you, I'm not going to Tok with you." She couldn't help looking curiously at the dogsled and team. "No matter how hard you try to entice me with adventurous modes of transportation." She turned back into the warmth of the house, not caring how grumpy she sounded this early on a weekend morning.

Kin followed her inside and closed the door, looking rueful as he watched her head back up the stairs to the loft. "And to think last night I was 'Kin.' "

"Maybe we can be friends when you start treating me with some respect and listen to what I tell you. You can let yourself out whenever you like. I'm going back to bed."

"Those poor dogs will get pretty chilly and uncomfortable if they have to sit out there for several hours while you get your beauty sleep. Totally unnecessary beauty sleep, I might add."

Concerned, she turned and looked down at him over the balcony railing. His words sounded sincere but the teasing glint in his eyes spoke volumes about his knowledge of her feeling for animals.

She gritted her teeth and gripped the railing. "Then take them home."

"Well, I suppose I could. But it'd be a real shame to disappoint them. They're all excited now about the prospect of hitting the open trail with all the fresh snow and everything . . ." His voice trailed off as he shook his head in melodramatic regret.

"Oh, all right!" Amanda surrendered. Turning on her slippered heel, she flounced into the loft bedroom and shut the door with a firm click.

Kin laughed and called out through the closed door, "Be sure you dress warmly."

When Amanda returned to the lower floor, she had traded her flannel nightgown and robe for long underwear covered by jeans and two bulky wool sweaters over a white turtleneck. She joined Kin in the kitchen where he was preparing a breakfast of scrambled eggs, bacon, toast, and hot chocolate. Her appearance was not stylish, but earned her a nod of approval.

He placed a plate of food and a cup of steaming cocoa on the breakfast bar. "How many pairs of socks do you have on? '

Sitting on a stool, she spread locally made blueberry jam on a piece of toast. "Three. I hope I can get my boots on." She watched him lounge against the sink. "Aren't you going to eat?"

Taking a few sips of his own cocoa, Kin put a few pots and pans in the dishwasher. "I already did. So did the team. It's your turn. You need hot food and drink in you before we hit the trail.'' He then proceeded to feed Frosty, who had been sitting patiently on the kitchen floor, painfully aware that the bacon and eggs were not for him.

As Amanda watched the hungry dog wolfing down his canned food, she remembered her plan to take him to a vet. ''Wait a minute. I was going to take Frosty to Tok with me.''

Kin wiped down the counters and stove with a damp dishrag. ''No problem. He's going with us.''

''In a dogsled?'' she asked incredulously.

''What better place for a dog?'' Kin chuckled at his own wit before continuing. ''Well, he can't run with the team. They all like to wear the same black-and-white uniform and he doesn't have one.'' He ruffled the animal's fur. ''So, he'll have to ride shotgun with you instead.''

A short time later, bundled and bulky, they made their way out to the sled. When Frosty made a beeline for the team, Kin quickly scooped him up, grabbed a rope from the sled, and tied it around the mutt's neck. The other end was attached to the back of the sled. ''It's best not to let him take their minds off the business at hand.''

He helped Amanda climb into the sled basket among the first aid and survival equipment stored there. Questioning her sanity for letting Kin talk her into doing this, she settled doubtfully into the basket. He untied Frosty and placed him in her lap, bundling a couple of thick wool blankets around them. His face was close to hers and their eyes met in a moment of shared excitement in anticipation of the adventure ahead of them. For a heartbeat, Amanda could almost believe there was hope that Kin would come to accept her presence in the bush.

Then he took his place on the runners at the back of the sled. "Mush!" he shouted into the dark morning. The team began moving as one, pulling the sled smoothly along at a rate of speed that picked up quickly when they left the center of Chena. They passed houses and the solitary log church before leaving the road and heading off through the frozen swamp on an unmarked trail that the dog team knew by heart.

Soon the heavy breathing of the animals and the swish of sled runners on fresh snow were the only sounds that softly broke the cold, dark silence. They made their way northwest across the frozen muskeg and Amanda was amazed at how easily the team avoided the scraggly black spruce trees scattered hither and yon throughout the area.

They had been on the trail for a couple of hours when a pale winter sun crept lazily over the horizon. It would make a short march across the sky before dropping out of sight again in a few hours. Kin donned a pair of dark glasses against the glare of the snow and offered Amanda a pair, which she gratefully accepted.

During their first stop, he produced a thermos of hot cocoa and some sandwiches packed in the sled. Amanda was surprised at how ravenous she felt, considering she had been sitting in the sled all morning.

Kin smiled as he watched her devour the peanut butter sandwich he had given her. "Fresh air creates quite an appetite, doesn't it?"

The gooey peanut butter rendering her temporarily mute, Amanda could only nod in agreement. ''Why peanut butter?'' she asked thickly after a few minutes.

''The fat is good in cold weather because shivering burns lots of energy. High-calorie, energy-giving foods are important to have out here. That's why chocolate is so great.'' He offered her a bright smile and a candy bar.

Snow fell like a lacy curtain around them as they resumed their trip. The quiet swishing sound of the runners was interrupted only by Kin's occasional call of ''Mush!'' Closing her eyes against the tree-laden muskeg, she allowed her mind to wander, weaving a fantasy of herself and Kin as Eskimos on a long trek across the Arctic tundra.

She was brought back to reality by a muttered oath from Kin as he put on the sled brake. Turning dreamily to look up at him, her eyes opened wide as he pulled his rifle from where it was secured at the back of the sled.

Spinning around to see what lay ahead that had caused Kin to prepare to shoot, Amanda's heart stopped momentarily. Long, bony legs supported a heavy, bulky body covered with brown hair. Large, soulful dark eyes watched the team curiously and a five-foot-wide rack of antlers pointed skyward, giving the bull moose a height of seven feet from hoof to antler tip.

Fascination and terror warred within Amanda, and she sat still, afraid to even breathe. At the same time, she was aware of the incongruous wish that she had thought to bring a camera.

A sudden movement and a low growl from Frosty

banished all thoughts from her mind except the necessity to keep him quiet. She gripped him tightly and grasped his snout like a vise. Though he quivered with excitement and twisted every which way in his quest for freedom, she held firm. He finally gave up the fight and simply watched the animal in the distance, a low, constant growl the only way he was able to make his disapproval known.

The dog team was on guard, each one quivering with excitement. Their beautiful coats bristled as they watched the bull. The moose was only about twenty feet ahead of the lead dog, Kodiak. Amanda had learned enough about wild animals to know that they must not startle or frighten the bull, lest he charge. It would kick and stomp all the dogs to death, and then go after her and Kin. The team was on its best behavior and she supposed they had had such encounters on the trail before.

Kin watched the animal warily, waiting, his rifle raised and aimed, ready to fire repeatedly should it be necessary. The chill north wind that had sprung up a short time earlier became more noticeable, intermittently blowing snow into their faces. Amanda shivered with a combination of cold and fear. Would the moose charge?

What was only a matter of about sixty seconds seemed like an eternity before the bull continued on his way across the trail to nibble on the branch of a tired old birch tree. After observing him for a short time, ensuring that he was more interested in his meal than in the travelers, Kin quietly ordered the team to "Mush!" The dogs sensed the firm command in his low tone and began pulling the sled slowly past the area where the moose was eating.

The big animal eyed them as he ate and Kin continued to hold his rifle in one mittened hand while grasping the sled handle with the other. They were about five hundred feet beyond the moose before he stopped the sled to secure the rifle and praise each furry member of the team in turn for their good behavior.

Upon approaching the sled again, he stopped and looked down at Amanda, admiration on his face and surprise in his voice. "You handled that encounter really well, Princess. We might make an Alaskan out of you yet." He earned a happy grin from her and patted her hooded head just as he had the dogs, before hopping back on the runners. They headed on along the peaceful white trail toward Tok.

Amanda basked in the warmth of his compliment, even though it sounded a trifle backhanded. He made it sound as if she would win his approval only if he could consider her worthy of the title "Alaskan." Still, she knew he was paying her a compliment and that he was impressed that she hadn't panicked. She wondered if her father would have given her the same credit for keeping a cool head, or if he would have said she was just speechless with fright. She suspected the latter.

The afternoon darkness had fallen again before they arrived in Tok. Kin drove the sled to the vet to leave the reluctant Frosty for a checkup and shots. He then pulled up in front of a large cabin built of peeled, varnished logs. As they climbed the wide steps to the porch, Amanda noticed a sign above the entrance that read "Warm-Up Hut."

Inside the store, Kin led Amanda past racks of outdoor clothing to a small wood-burning stove at the back of the room. While she warmed herself by the stove, Amanda allowed her gaze to wander over the racks of parkas, colorful snowsuits, and fashionable ski suits. Thick, multicolored sweaters sat in neat piles on modern acrylic shelves that were totally incongruous with the rustic interior of the cabin. The walls were lined with wooden shelves packed with various types of boots, including mukluks and balloonish white "bunny" boots.

Everything imaginable was available for cold weather and outdoor recreation. Hooks on the walls displayed backpacks and canvas bags. There were skis, ski poles, snowshoes, sleds, and even toboggans.

Amanda turned to find Kin in light conversation with the proprietor, a tall, angular man of about fifty, with a beakish nose and kind blue eyes behind horn-rimmed glasses.

Kin took her arm and drew her forward. "Amanda, this is George Sarkles. He owns the Warm-Up Hut. George, Amanda Roberts, Chena's new teacher from the Lower Forty-eight."

A warm, firm handshake welcomed Amanda to Tok. The proprietor glanced down at the impractical leather boots covering her feet, and the jeans tucked clumsily inside. "Kin tells me you're in need of some serious winter outfitting. Shall we start with a pair of warm boots?"

Amanda and Kin left the Warm-Up Hut laden with bags containing a pair of nylon snow pants and her old boots. She had opted to wear the comfortable caribou-hide mukluks just purchased at the cost of an arm and a leg. After loading the packages and Amanda into the sled, Kin pointed the team in the direction of a large grocery store.

The brightly lit interior of the supermarket beckoned Amanda as Kin held the door for her to enter. "We don't have much room left in the sled, but if you see a few things you want, we can still fit them in."

Amanda was thrilled that a small town like Tok would contain such a large grocery store. She actually felt a trifle overwhelmed by the size and bright lights after a week of shopping in the small, crowded general store. Kin reminded her that Tok was a major crossroads between Anchorage, Fairbanks, and the Yukon Territory on the Alaska Highway, which he called the Alcan.

She fell to her task with zeal, dragging him up and down every aisle twice before deciding upon a limited supply of items his store either did not carry, or sold at a much higher price. As if daring him to come up with an answer that would satisfy her, she stopped in the frozen food aisle and looked him sternly in the eye. "Why are your prices in Chena so much higher than these?"

"Chena is way off the main road running between Anchorage and Fairbanks. It costs me a lot more to have delivery trucks go to Chena than it would if my store were here in Tok." With a glance into the freezer that held ice cream and other frozen confections, he went on. "And if you want that ice cream, go ahead. You've hauled me past here four times, and it's beginning to make me cold. We'll just leave it on the sled and I guarantee it won't melt.''

Peppermint ice cream was a delicacy unavailable in Chena, so Amanda picked up a carton and headed for the checkout line, speaking to Kin over her shoulder. ''Where else would we put it but on the sled? It's not as if we'll be indoors anywhere between here and Chena tonight.''

There was a momentary pause before Kin replied. ''Some of your things we'll take inside for the night.''

Amanda skidded to a halt as his intent sank in. She turned to face him warily, and her next words sounded like chips of ice. ''For the night? What do you mean? We're heading back home soon, aren't we?''

''Mandy, it's dark and the temperature is dropping. The team is tired and hungry and so am I. We're spending the night in Tok.''

She stared in outrage at his impassive countenance. ''Not . . . I . . . you . . .'' Unable to form a coherent sentence, she stomped one muklukked foot furiously and carried her grocery basket to the shortest line.

After paying for her purchases, Amanda walked to a pay phone to thumb through a telephone directory the size of a *Reader's Digest.*

Kin heaved a sigh behind her. ''What are you doing?''

She turned to spare him a hot glare before continuing her search through the phone book. ''I'm looking into the city bus situation to see how soon I can catch one heading toward Chena.''

His shout of laughter drew surprised glances from store patrons and clerks. ''You're on the edge of the

Alaska bush in the middle of winter. There are no city buses here, even in summer. And at this time of year, you couldn't even find a tour bus to hookeybob on.''

Temporarily distracted from her mission, she looked at him. ''Hookeybob, did you say?'' she echoed faintly.

''That's when you squat down behind a vehicle and grab the rear bumper. You slide along on the ice behind it as it drives. It's a very dangerous game kids play with school buses in the winter.'' He enjoyed the look of dawning amazement that replaced the anger on her face as she listened.

With a puzzled shake of her head, Amanda decided there was no alternative but to accompany Kin wherever he chose to go. She dropped the phone directory in disgust and picked up her purchases to head for the door. She refused to allow Kin to carry her bag to the sled. Staring straight ahead, she avoided his eyes as he tucked blankets around her before he stepped onto the runners and called, ''Mush!''

Of course the team is tired and hungry, she thought irritably as they crossed the highway during a break in traffic. *But Kin had to have known we'd be spending the night here when he showed up at my house this morning. This was his plan. He never had any intention of making the round trip in one day. He knew it would be dark and the team tired when we got here. After all, it's not as though this is his first sled trip to Tok. Yet, he never even hinted that we'd spend the night. He knows I don't know anything about dog sledding and caring for a team. And he certainly knows that I expected to go home today, because he knows I'd planned to drive here. He intentionally tricked me, so I'd look like I can't take care of myself.*

While the innocent dog team was deserving of her concern and sympathy, Kincaid Russell was not. This whole thing had been his idea in the first place. All she had wanted was to take a leisurely day trip to Tok and then home again in her car. He had played on her sense of adventure with the dogsled, and on her feelings for animals when he talked about the team looking forward to the trip. Why, the man was just plain devious!

When the sled stopped in front of the vet's office, Amanda shoved the blankets off and tumbled out of the basket and up the porch steps to the door. She did not deign to glance back at Kin. Of course, he probably found the entire situation very amusing. After all, his trick had worked like a charm. *So far,* she thought with determination.

Frosty greeted Amanda as if he hadn't seen her in years. When she rejoined Kin outside, he was ruffling the coats of some of the huskies and telling them their long day would soon be over. Upon looking up to find Amanda's frown directed at him, he merely lifted one eyebrow and took his place on the runners. He didn't even offer to help her into the sled.

With the wriggling burden of Frosty in her arms, Amanda found the sled basket more difficult to negotiate this time. The dog was trying to crawl over her shoulder to greet Kin, and Amanda was half in and half out of the basket when he unceremoniously grabbed her under the arms from behind and hauled her backward into the sled.

He patted the delighted animal. ''Hey, Frosty, old boy.'' Then, ''Mush!'', and they were moving along the dirty roadside snow toward a housing development.

It had stopped snowing a couple of hours earlier. The sky had cleared and the temperature was dropping. Tiny ice crystals glittered in the dark air under the streetlights as they made their way to an attractive split-level house. Surrounding it was a six-foot wooden fence made several inches higher by the buildup of fresh snow.

Kin stopped the sled in the driveway. ''This is George Sarkles's home. I stay here if I'm ever in Tok for the night, which is rare.''

''He seems like a very nice man,'' Amanda said in a subdued tone. Guilt assailed her at the uncharitable direction her thoughts had taken.

They were greeted at the door by a plump, rosy-cheeked woman with short, curly iron-gray hair and a ready smile for the orange mutt in Amanda's arms.

''Maddie, this is Amanda Roberts,'' Kin said, only to have the woman pull them inside the house.

She closed the door behind them and rubbed her chilly arms. ''No sense in heating the great outdoors,'' she said in a jovial tone. ''George called and said you were on your way. It's so good to see you again, Kin.'' With a warm smile for Amanda, she rambled cheerfully on. ''He said you're a new teacher from Outside. How do you like Alaska, dear?''

''Well, I—''

''But we'll talk about all that at dinner when George gets home,'' the woman gushed. She turned back to Kin. ''You can set the team up in the backyard, Kin. They must be pretty hungry after a day on the trail. And this little fellow,'' she said with a pat for Frosty, ''can stay in the house.''

While Kin nodded and let himself back outside, Maddie took Frosty from Amanda and set him on the floor. ''Dinner will be on the table when George gets home. Take off your things and come in by the fire to warm up, dear.''

''Actually, I should help Kin with the team and then we can all get comfortable faster.'' Amanda glanced at Frosty, who was busily sniffing every inch of the living room, his shaggy tail wagging periodically when some scent pleased him. ''Can I leave him with you?''

Maddie nodded. ''Oh, yes, run along, run along. I'll be in the kitchen and I'm sure he'll join me there.'' She waved a hand and Amanda went out the door.

Kin was shoveling snow away from the fence gate so the huskies could enter the backyard. He looked up in surprise when she arrived to help, but neither of them said anything. He continued shoveling while she pushed on the gate, opening it inch by stubborn inch until the built-up ice prevented it from going any further. Amanda created a wide-enough space for the animals to go through in half the time it would have taken Kin to do it alone, and couldn't help giving him an arch look when he smiled his thanks.

Once the team was inside the fence, Kin unharnessed the dogs so they could run around the yard, wrestle, play, and dig for interesting smells in the snow. Amanda followed his lead in preparing their food and water.

They were watching the huskies eat when she decided she needed to know the truth about his plans. "Why didn't you tell me this morning that we'd be spending the night in Tok?"

"Because I knew you wouldn't come with me if I told you."

"Why was that so important?" Shame assailed her at the knowledge that she wanted him to say something about his feelings for her. Considering how he felt about cheechakos, she should walk away and leave him in the cold. Literally and figuratively!

But she didn't want to think about that. They had just worked well together, opening the gate. It had been hard work and the temperature was bitter, yet even he couldn't deny she had done a good job. Maybe his opinion of her as a helpless "fashion princess" would change.

Kin led two of the dogs to a corner by the back wall of the house to bed them down. "You needed a trip like this. Something to break you in, out here in the bush. You needed to see how harsh it can be."

"Why? So I'll turn tail and run home to Mommy and Daddy?"

"Not necessarily. But you may decide to run home to the Lower Forty-eight."

So it *was* a test. He continued to wage his campaign to get rid of the cheechako schoolteacher. She had been hoping he was coming to accept her. Obviously, she'd been mistaken.

"Sorry to disappoint you, but I'm not going anywhere."

"Did I say I'm disappointed?"

She felt tears sting her eyes. "Why bother?" An

abrupt change of subject seemed in order. "Do the dogs have to stay out here all night? It's awful cold."

He watched some of the dogs curl up to sleep while others began licking and chewing the ice from their paws. "They're huskies, Princess. They're tough outdoor animals. They live outside all the time. At home they have doghouses. But they often choose to sleep on the tops of their houses or in the snow. Don't worry, they're fine. They're in their element."

They headed for the door to the garage and Amanda wrinkled her nose in confusion. "How does a dog sleep on top of a doghouse? Don't they slide down the roof?"

"No. The roofs are flat, so it's easy. I build the doghouses like square boxes." Kin held the door for her and they entered the garage just as an old blue pickup pulled in. They waited for George to step out of the truck and close the garage door.

"Team all settled, Kin?"

"Yes, they're happy to be visiting again. I'll check on them before I hit the hay." Kin winked devilishly at Amanda and she wanted to sink through the floor in embarrassment. She had no secrets from him. He knew she thought he had planned a big seduction for tonight.

Maddie was putting dinner on the table when they entered the house. They all sat around the shining oak dining table to enjoy a succulent moose roast with potatoes and gravy.

Amanda learned from the Sarkleses that Tok started as a settlement when construction was begun on the Alaska Highway by the Army Corps of Engineers in 1942. At that time, the Alaska Railroad Commission set up Tokyo Camp near the Tokyo River. The names were shortened to Tok due to sentiments brought about during World War II.

Kin begged to differ with the Sarkleses' version of how Tok got its name. Athabascan Indian legend, he said, told of how the Tokai River, later renamed the Tok River, was a place where tribes gathered for peace, and the word Tokai meant "peace crossing."

"At any rate, it's a major crossroads for the state," George said with a chuckle when they agreed to disagree on how Tok got its name.

The long day in the cold air left Amanda tired enough to want to go to bed early. Maddie showed her to a guest room upstairs while explaining that Kin used a room in the basement.

The room had belonged to one of the Sarkleses' grown daughters and still retained her youthful stamp in the yellow-and-white striped wallpaper, splashed with flowers and leaves. Maddie cleared numerous stuffed animals and a threadbare Raggedy Ann off the bed and closed buttery yellow corduroy curtains against the cold, dark night. A long flannel nightgown and fleecy robe accompanied the thick towels she gave Amanda.

She showed Amanda the adjoining bathroom and went to turn down the bed. "Have a nice hot soak in the tub and call if you need anything. You and Kin will have to come again soon. We miss having the girls come around with their friends, now that they both live in Anchorage. It's nice to have young sweethearts in the house again."

"Oh, but Kin and I aren't sweethearts." An embarrassed Amanda remembered with a pang the kisses they had shared.

"No? But I could have sworn . . ." Maddie looked closely at Amanda's flushed countenance before displaying a slow, secretive smile. "I see," she murmured.

Amanda had a feeling Maddie saw more than was really there but decided against trying to explain her strained friendship with Kin. As she prepared for her bath, she considered how the population of Chena would react if it was discovered that they had spent a night together in Tok. She didn't care for the thought of her name being connected with Kin's in juicy and inaccurate speculative gossip. And what about Lucinda? If she and Kin were romantically involved, this overnight trip with Amanda could cause problems.

The hot tub of water, scented with wild rose, was blissful to her tired body after a day in the freezing outdoors. Her mind wandered over the events of the day and she had to admit that a warm bath and bed were infinitely more pleasant for passing the night than riding back to Chena in Kin's dogsled.

The flannel nightie was soft and warm, and Amanda felt pleasantly sleepy when she turned out the light. Burrowing under the warm covers, she vaguely wondered what on earth had given Maddie the idea that she and Kin were sweethearts, before she slipped into a deep sleep.

She dreamed that a gentle and loving man held her warmly, caressing her cheeks with soft, sweet kisses and whispering her name with love in his voice. He stroked her tangled hair and she snuggled against him with a contented sigh.

Then his repeated whispering of her name became more insistent, and he shook her. When she awoke with a start, it was to find Kin sitting on her bed in the dark room.

Chapter Six

The dim glow of a hall nightlight seeped in and her heart pounded. The realization that Kin was the man in her lovely dream caused Amanda's cheeks to flame. She pushed him away and tried to erase the memory of the dream from her mind as she tugged at the bedcovers.

"What are you doing in here?"

His dark eyes glittered with excitement. "Get up and put on your robe. There's something I want you to see outside."

She looked at him as if he'd lost his mind. "Are you crazy? I'm not going out in that freezing air in the middle of the night. Thanks to you, I spent the whole day out there." Shaking her head, she tried again to push him away. "You're nuts. What time is it, anyway?"

"It's midnight. And you *are* going out there with

me if I have to carry you. Now hurry up and get ready. I'd hate for you to awaken George and Maddie with a tantrum, because what I have to show you is something they've seen a hundred times. Put on your robe and socks and meet me in the hall. I promise you won't be sorry.'' He let himself out into the dark hall.

A grumpy Amanda donned the robe over her nightie and, after pulling on her socks, slowly peered into the hall. In the murky light, she saw Kin, who took her by the hand to the closet where their parkas hung. Too sleepy to argue anymore, she allowed him to bundle her into her parka and mukluks before he quickly donned his own.

Taking her hand again, he led her down the stairs to the front door. The freezing air woke her completely when he pulled her out onto the porch.

She stared in awe at the magnificent night sky. ''What in . . .''

Like drifting folds of colorful curtains, light shone and moved gently in the dark, clear sky. Mostly green and pink in color, with shades of yellow and blue, the huge curtains of light varied in intensity and movement as they spread across the night sky.

''It must be—''

''The northern lights.'' He placed his strong hands on her shoulders and stood directly behind her. ''I didn't think you'd ever seen a sight like this. I was checking the team when they started. They've just been growing and brightening since then.''

Folding curtains of light continued to grow in size, their color intensifying. The spectacle spread further across the sky, extending from about sixty miles above the earth, high into space.

Amanda shivered in the penetrating cold and watched the ethereal display, returning to reality with a thud when Kin embraced her from behind, hugging her close against his broad chest so he could rest his chin atop her head. She longed to entwine her arms around his neck and press her face against his. Instead, she allowed herself to relax against him and his arms tightened.

As if he had read her mind, he turned her toward him and lowered his mouth to hers in a warm, sweet kiss. Her arms crept up around his neck, pulling his face closer, as she had longed to do.

Soon she pulled weakly out of his warm embrace and gazed up at him. "I'd better go inside now."

He gripped her arms momentarily before releasing her, and turned to open the door. With a last look at the light show in the sky, Amanda stepped into the warmth of the house and unzipped the heavy parka. She moved up the stairs to put it away in the closet with the mukluks.

In the darkness, she turned to face him. "Thank you for showing me the lights," she whispered.

His gaze took in her powder-blue fleece robe and white nightie, and he lifted a hand to touch her cheek for a tender moment. White teeth flashed in the darkness. "Good night, sweet Mandy." He turned and went down the stairs to his room in the basement.

Amanda stared after him, the sudden pain in her heart almost too much to bear. She rushed into her room and closed the door firmly, leaning against it as if she could hold off all the overwhelming feelings.

When she awoke early the next morning, Kin was already outside harnessing the team for the long trip back to Chena. She dressed quickly while Maddie prepared breakfast, and was telling Maddie and George about the previous night's light show when Kin entered the house and came into the kitchen, rubbing his cold hands together.

George took a sip of coffee. "I understand you've taken to pulling young women out of bed in the middle of the night for sight-seeing, Kin."

Kin grinned, pulled off his parka, and hung it over the back of a chair. "Only when they're worthwhile."

"The sights or the women?"

Kin smiled more broadly. "What do you think?"

Amanda lowered her head to concentrate on buttering a piece of toast as she relived in her mind the warm embrace they'd shared the night before.

Seating himself at the breakfast table, Kin speared a couple of rashers of bacon off a heaping platter and looked at her. "Mandy, the temperature has dropped considerably since yesterday afternoon. We may have to take it a little slower, what with the windchill factor. You'll be less comfortable, but we'll get there just fine."

"Kin will take good care of you, dear," Maddie assured her kindly.

Amanda watched Kin across the table. "I know he will." Surprise at the realization that she meant it gave her pause. It was true; she could trust Kin with her life. Trusting him with her heart was what gave her misgivings. Though that shouldn't even be an issue, she was too honest not to admit it had become one.

It was still dark when Kin tucked the old wool blankets snugly around Amanda and Frosty in the sled. Amanda and Kin both had wool scarves wrapped around their noses and mouths, and she felt a pang of guilt as she watched him. Hoarfrost had built up on every outdoor surface overnight. Tree branches looked lacy and delicate, blanketed in the frost caused by brutal subzero temperatures. Knowing Kin would be standing on the runners while she enjoyed relative comfort made her feel like a heel.

Concern showed in Kin's eyes as he instructed her through the scarf covering his mouth. "Tell me whenever you become too uncomfortable. I plan to stop frequently."

Amanda nodded, his thoughtfulness making her feel even more guilty. He would bear the brunt of the chill factor as he drove the sled. A warm sparkle lit his eyes and he squeezed her shoulder before rising to take his place on the runners.

George and Maddie waved and called out their good-byes from the front door while Kin waved back and shouted, "Mush!"

During their first stop, Frosty explored while Amanda helped Kin with the team. The brightly colored mutt sniffed further and further into the surrounding trees, causing Kin to comment, "Don't lose sight of him. A moose would make short work of him."

Such a threat to her lovable pet induced Amanda to call him back to the sled. Ignoring his yips of protest and the injured look in his soulful brown eyes, she tied him up. Rejoining Kin in his labors with the team, she expressed an idea that had occurred to her when they departed Tok.

"Maybe you can show me how to drive the team."

Kin straightened and pulled his frost-encrusted scarf away from his face, grinning broadly. "I'd planned on teaching you how to drive a car first."

She punched him playfully on the arm. "Just because I don't speed on one-way bridges like some people is no reason to get smart."

Kin looked serious now. "Princess, these are not the kind of conditions I would choose to teach you to drive a sled in."

"It can't be that hard."

He frowned. "There is certainly a technique to driving a dog team. Do you mind telling me why it's so important that you learn now?"

She glanced at the blankets in the basket. "I just thought if I knew . . . that it would be a good idea. What if you got hurt and couldn't drive? I really need to know."

Kin followed her gaze, then took her mittened hands in his own and held them tightly, giving her a gentle smile. "Sweet Mandy, what am I going to do with you? Listen, I was born and raised in this bush. I cut my teeth on real icicles. I'm always prepared for conditions like this. Heck, I bet you I'm more comfortable on the back of a sled in this weather than you are underneath all those blankets. We have a lot of miles to cover and it's well below zero out here. You are much more at risk in this weather than I am. The important thing is for us to get back to the village as quickly as possible. That means I am the coachman and you are the princess. Understand?"

Unable to argue with his logic, she nodded reluctantly. He looked into her face a moment longer, then turned to prepare the dogs and sled for another stretch on the trail to Chena.

They were both ravenous when they finally stopped for lunch. Kin built a small campfire on the side of the trail and they devoured the roast moose sandwiches and thermos of hot chocolate Maddie had sent with them as they enjoyed the heat.

A smile crept over Amanda's face while she warmed her hands over the flames. "I wish I could take my boots and socks off and put my bare feet over the fire." She gave Kin a curious look. "You really thrive on this lifestyle, don't you?"

"It was all I knew until I went away to college in the Lower Forty-eight."

"Did you ever consider not coming back?"

"Sure. Who wouldn't? But, I guess I love life out here more than any other place. Life is a challenge in the bush." He finished his cocoa before adding solemnly, "And I have an obligation to my family and the tribe."

"You sound like you expect to be the next big chief."

An odd look entered his eyes, and he smiled and stood, pulling her to her feet so quickly she almost lost her balance and had to grip his arms for support. After smothering the campfire, they made their way back to the sled.

They had only traveled a few miles when Kin stopped again and walked forward to one of the huskies running just ahead of the sled. He patted the animal and spoke quietly, lifting her left hind leg to examine the foot pads. Turning to Amanda, who was watching from the basket, he looked apologetic.

"Do you and Frosty mind another houseguest on the Chena Express?"

"Houseguest?"

"Galena should ride. She's lame."

"That's fine. But will you be able to drive the sled with half the population of Chena in it? Will the others still be able to pull?" Before he could answer, she went on decidedly, "I guess this is my chance to get out on those runners with you."

His eyes shone. "I'd like that a lot. But it's not necessary. The other six dogs will do fine. They're used to pulling heavy loads." The matter was closed as far as he was concerned.

It didn't take long to unharness and regroup the dogs. When he turned to settle Galena in the basket, Kin found Amanda standing next to the runners.

"I'm ready when you are," she said.

He regarded her steadily for a moment, about to say "No." Instead, he sighed and gave her a crooked grin. "Seems I can't deny you anything."

Kin settled Galena and Frosty, allowing them time to sniff each other and come to some sort of doggy understanding. Frosty curled up next to the husky and rested his chin on her back with a contented look on his face.

Kin joined Amanda on the back of the sled. "Looks like we can trust them not to go into battle." Placing a hand on each side of her waist, he moved her into position behind the runners. "Stand with one foot on each runner and hold the handlebar firmly with both hands." After she followed his directions, he stepped behind her on the runners. Then he reached around her, one arm on each side, to grasp the bar with one hand and the gangline running from the sled to the dogs' lines with the other.

"This was a great idea. I could get used to riding this way. I'll take you along on every sled ride from now on," he murmured.

Warm breath fanned her cheek and she feigned a coolness she was far from feeling while his strong arms imprisoned her on the runners. "We'd better go. It's getting late," she replied in a shaky voice.

An aggrieved sigh preceded his next instructions. "If we must. Hang on with both hands all the time. I'll do the driving." Amanda lurched against him as he called, "Mush!" and shoved off with one foot, bracing her more securely on the runners by tightening his arms.

Once the sled picked up speed, gliding over the crusty snow toward Chena, Amanda felt alternate thrills of exhilaration and fear. Riding the runners was less secure and more invigorating than riding in the basket. The feel of Kin's arms around her and his hands on the bar next to hers allowed for no relaxation.

She laughed with delight as they went down a slight incline. "This is fun!"

His arms tightened perceptibly on each side of her. "You're a good sport, Mandy."

An attempt at mind over matter allowed Amanda to ignore her pounding pulse while examining the tumultuous feelings she had for Kin. She heartily wished he didn't have a prejudice against Outsiders. The relationship between them had improved dramatically, yet he remained unable to recognize her strength. He still cherished the belief that she had no staying power here in the bush, as evidenced by his admission last night that this trip was a test.

The longing for him to accept her as an equal who could handle life in the wild with zeal and self-sufficiency was overwhelming. She wanted his approval. What she felt for Kin was beyond casual, beyond friendship, and it was frightening because, without his acceptance, she was headed for heartbreak. Telling herself she had to avoid Kin for self-protection, her body stiffened inadvertently.

Kin seemed to sense the change in her posture. "What is it? What's wrong?"

"Nothing. Keep going."

"Are you cold? Do you want to get back into the basket?"

"Maybe that would be best," she rasped.

Kin brought the team to a halt and frowned when Amanda jumped off the runners as if they were red-hot. She climbed into the basket behind the two happily snoozing dogs and he gazed at her intently while tucking the blankets around her. She schooled her features into an impassive mask and refused to meet his eyes.

He put a mittened hand to her rosy, chapped cheek. "Want to talk about it?"

"No. Let's go," she said tersely.

He sat on his haunches for another minute, frowning at her. "It's all going to work out, you know." His quiet assurance made her wonder as he stood and moved again to the back of the sled.

The rest of the trip passed in silence. Amanda

thought about Kin's words and wondered what he knew about her concerns. It would be too humiliating for him to guess how she felt about him. Dealing with his disdain for her as a cheechako was bad enough without him figuring out where her heart lay.

The afternoon sun was setting with a warm alpenglow, painting the snow-covered landscape a cotton-candy pink, when they arrived in Chena. They stopped in front of Amanda's house and she tumbled out of the sled. After quickly unloading some of her belongings, she trudged to the door with them.

Kin watched in silence for a moment, lines of puzzlement creasing his brow before he picked up the items she had dropped in the snow during her rush to get to the door—her rush to get away from him.

She fumbled in her satchel for the house key. "It was very nice of you to take me to Tok, Kin. Thank you for the unique mode of transportation. I don't want to keep you from the other obligations you most certainly have."

He shook his head and was equally formal as he reached around her to unlock the door with a key of his own. "You're welcome and you won't."

Amanda entered the house and turned to stare at him. "You have a key to my house?"

His mouth twisted cynically. "*My* house. And, yes, I do. Don't tell me nobody has ever had a key to your house before."

"That's none of your business," she replied indignantly. "And I would appreciate it if you didn't use that key when I am around." She felt his mocking eyes boring into her and was conscious of the dry, red patches of windburn left on her cheeks from yesterday's ride.

"Wouldn't think of it. I have no doubt you'll always welcome me whenever I come to your door."

His words were casual enough, but his tone spoke volumes. He was fully aware of her increasing interest in him, and her sporadic attempts at formality didn't fool him in the least.

"Don't be so sure of yourself, Mr. Russell. I never play second best for any man."

He watched her toss packages on the couch. "So I'm Mr. Russell again, huh? And what do you mean by 'second best'?"

"Think about it and I'm sure you'll figure it out." She strode blindly past him to collect Frosty and the rest of her belongings from the sled. Frosty ran around, sniffing his familiar territory, and she had to call him several times before he came to the house.

When she entered the house again, Kin was in the kitchen, fooling with the faucet. Hearing her come in, he turned around, slipping a small piece of paper into his pocket. "I was checking to see if the pipes froze during your absence." He spoke casually. "It's been terribly cold."

"I can check things. I'll call you if anything goes haywire. Now, I'm sure Galena would like to get home and have some TLC, and that the whole team is eager to be unharnessed."

Her blatant invitation for him to leave caused him to raise an eyebrow. "Can't argue with that. Do you want to come with me now, or shall I pick you up a little later?"

Amanda felt the leash on her temper being strained.

Now what was he planning? Did he think she was going to spend the evening with him even after the last couple of hours were spent forcing herself to give him the cold shoulder? She had to get rid of him and have time alone to think. There had to be a way of handling her feelings for him without all these dramatic mood changes.

"Neither, thank you," she said with what she considered admirable patience. "I have things to do and I have to get ready for school tomorrow. So, I'll be seeing you around, okay?"

"Around my house, yes."

The leash snapped. "What on earth is the matter with you? I don't plan on going anywhere else today. Certainly not to your house. Can I make myself any clearer than that?"

"Mandy, your pipes are frozen. You can't stay here until I get them fixed."

She frowned at him in disbelief. "They can't be frozen. We weren't gone that long. They were fine yesterday morning." Hurrying past him to the kitchen sink, she uselessly turned the faucets on and off, willing water to come out. It didn't.

"The temperature dropped way below zero and you didn't leave the faucet dripping, so the pipes froze."

"Of course I didn't leave them dripping. That's a terrible waste of water."

"Hardly a big concern in Alaska," he responded dryly.

"Well, I'll just stay here without running water. I . . . I'll melt snow on the stove." Having said it, she warmed to the idea. "Yeah. That'll be a kick. I'll be like a pioneer or something."

"Mandy, you can't stay here. The frozen pipes could burst and flood the house. I'll get someone in to start work on it in the morning if I can. Meanwhile, you'll have to stay at my house till it's taken care of."

"Your house? No way. I'll stay at the lodge."

"There are no rooms available at the lodge," he countered quickly.

"Ha! Of course there are rooms at this time of year. Why, I'm sure every single room in the lodge is now available. And there's nothing you can do about it." She smirked. "I didn't notice the lodge parking area was swamped with cars when we arrived, did you?"

"I own the lodge and if I say there are no rooms available, that means there are no rooms available."

Amanda's face fell. "You can't do that."

"Sure I can. At the lodge, we reserve the right to refuse service to anyone. Look, I have a big house and I live in it alone. There is no reason you can't use one of the bedrooms," he said, pretending to twirl a long moustache, "while you wait for the pipes to be fixed."

She didn't miss the wicked gleam in his eye and knew he did it on purpose just to discomfit her. For that reason alone, she sounded deliberately offhanded when she replied, "Fine. I'll stay at your house. I'm overwhelmed by your generous offer of assistance, since there is no room at the inn. According to your edict, that is. But how will it look if I move into your house?"

His eyes glinted like steel. "As I said, I live alone. I don't need permission from anyone to have a houseguest. Now, do you want some time to get ready to move or do you want to come with me right away?''

''I'd like some time, thanks.''

''Fine. I'll take the team home and get them taken care of, then I'll be back to pick you up.''

Suddenly, she felt very tired and was willing to give in to anything. These verbal sparring matches with him took a lot out of her. ''I have my own car. How do I find your house?''

''Just follow the Chena road east, around past the lodge, and you'll eventually see it. It's about a mile and it's the biggest house in the village.''

''You live alone in the biggest house in the village? Bigger even than your own chief's? Well, that makes a whole lot of sense.''

''I don't plan on living in it alone forever,'' he said meaningfully. ''I didn't build it with that in mind.''

She had the grace to blush at her shrewish attitude. ''Of course not. I'm sorry for being so difficult. I promise to be a polite houseguest.''

''I have no doubt of it. See you in an hour, okay? Call if you need any help. With luck, this will only be for a couple of days, so don't worry about it too much.''

Don't worry, he says. After he left, Amanda sat down on the couch, staring around at her home. She thought back over her weekend with Kin, the time on the trail, and the embrace on the Sarkleses' porch the night before. Now, she was supposed to live in his house for a couple of days, her heart in closer proximity to him than ever before, and he said not to worry.

Tears ran silently down her cheeks. Kin believed

she was a wimpy "fashion princess" who would never cut it in the bush. Even if she overcame that obstacle in some small way, there was still that nagging question about his relationship with Lucinda. Was there any substance to Elly's belief that Kin and Lucinda were romantically involved?

All day, she had warily circled the knowledge that she was both happier and more miserable than she had ever been in her life. How could something so intense and lasting happen so quickly? Yet, it had. She was deeply in love with Kincaid Russell. And he had no use for her, whatsoever, except possibly as a source of amusement.

Somehow, she had to force herself to hide the depth of her feelings for him. But how to do that while living under the same roof with him? Seeing him every morning, afternoon, and evening in the intimate surroundings of his home would only make it harder to keep her distance. She would have to tread very carefully and keep her feelings at bay during the next couple of days. He mustn't suspect how she felt or it would be too easy for him to take advantage and then leave her nursing the pain, knowing he didn't return those feelings.

It wasn't that she didn't believe Kin had feelings for her. He really seemed to care in his own, flirtatious way. He had been kind to her, and concerned that she be comfortable in Chena, once he began making a small effort to accept the fact that she wasn't leaving immediately. But nothing erased Lucinda from the picture.

As she went about packing a few things, Amanda steeled herself to be cool and impersonal toward Kin during her time in his house. Not for one minute did she think it was going to be easy. After all, she had tried so many times already to put up a wall against him, and he always walked right through it, into her arms.

Chapter Seven

Kin's house was indeed easy to spot. Amanda admired the log cabin, which was similar in style to other cabins in the village, but larger and more attractive with gabled windows on the second story. Built on sturdy stilts, it had a wide front porch enclosed by a log railing, and picture windows faced out across the porch and snow-covered muskeg.

The front door opened when she drove up, and Kin bounded down the steps to greet her. Her heart skipped a few beats as she admired his lean frame clad in fresh jeans and a white turtleneck, which set off the glow of his copper skin and the sheen of his neat black hair.

She stepped out of her car, followed by an excited Frosty. "You should have a coat on. It's way below zero out here," she chided.

Kin's teeth flashed white to match his pullover as

he gave her a teasing grin. "Yes, Mother." He opened the back of her station wagon and grabbed her suitcase.

Amanda surreptitiously glanced in all directions to see if anyone was watching. It just didn't look right for the new schoolteacher in this tiny village to be entering the home of Chena's most eligible bachelor with a suitcase. She quickly grabbed Hailey the Hippo and a sack of dog food, calling to Frosty as she followed Kin to the house. She noticed a moose rack mounted at the tip of the pointed roof over the porch, another of Kin's hunting trophies.

They entered the house, and Kin took her to the living room, where the centerpiece was a huge stone fireplace. A crackling fire was reflected in the varnished birch occasional tables scattered about the room. Amanda knew she would feel completely comfortable in the spacious but cozy home if only she didn't have reservations about her feelings for Kin. The warm house reflected the man, and she loved the man.

They walked down a hall with a shining hardwood floor to a lovely bedroom decorated in accents of rose and gray. Placing her suitcase on the bed, Kin turned to her with a smile.

"This will be your room. I'm right next door if you need anything."

"This is lovely." She set Hailey on the bed. "I'll be just fine."

"Good. Now, why don't you unpack while I go out back to feed the team? Make yourself at home, explore the house, have some coffee or whatever. I'll be back inside in half an hour."

He started to leave the room but turned back, taking her face in his weather-roughened hands and pressing his lips to hers in a warm kiss. Raising his mouth, he touched his dark forehead to her fair one. His eyes were unreadable, but she found herself imagining for a moment that he shared her feelings. *Oh, if only . . .*

"Just remember, never say never, sweet Mandy." His words were a velvet murmur. "Some things are beyond our power to stop. True love is one of those things. You can't stop the real thing." Brushing his lips over hers once more, he turned and left the room.

Amanda gasped and sat down hard on the bed next to her suitcase. For the second time that day she was unable to trust her trembling legs. Was Kin hinting that he suspected how she felt about him? He couldn't know exactly but must certainly be aware of her attraction to him. How was she going to keep her love a secret while living under his roof?

It didn't take long to unpack the few things she'd brought, and she was soon able to wander through the rest of the house, seeing Kin's stamp everywhere in the rustic dwelling. A large study was filled with books and a rolltop desk that, though neat, was stacked with papers and files. She'd never thought of Kin as being an avid reader, but the bookshelves were packed with books of all kinds and every imaginable subject matter. Sitting in an oversized leather wingback chair, she wondered idly if he'd ever considered adding local librarian to his list of jobs, before losing herself in a volume of irreverent poetry by the Bard of the Yukon, Robert Service.

"I forgot I have a bookworm for a houseguest."

With a startled jump and a guilty look, Amanda looked up from *The Ballad of Blasphemous Bill* to find Kin standing nearby. The warmth of his smile almost melted her heart and she made a great show of closing the book while she tried to calm her racing pulse.

"I guess I lost track of time."

Running a finger along the spine of the hardcover, Kin said, "Service is timeless." Then he took the book from her and set it on his desk, pulling her to her feet with his other hand. "My stomach, on the other hand, runs on a loudly ticking clock. Let's think about food now and literature later, okay?"

"I've been exploring your house. I mean, I did explore it before I found the library," Amanda told him on the way to the kitchen. "It's lovely. Did you build it yourself?"

Kin nodded as they entered the cheerfully decorated kitchen, where white appliances were offset by copper utensils that gleamed against sunny yellow walls. "Yes, several years ago. I'm glad you like it. Very glad."

His warm eyes lingered on her face and Amanda dropped her gaze to Frosty as he padded in and proceeded to sniff along under the cupboards for any stray crumbs. Her tone was strained even as she tried to sound nonchalant. "So the team is all taken care of?"

"Yes. And you and I are going to the lodge for dinner." His gaze followed hers to the busy dog. "Has he eaten?"

"I fed him before coming over here. He's just sniffing around because he doesn't want any stray crumbs to go uncollected. He's very neat and tidy, you see.'' She studiously avoided Kin's gaze as she spoke, her eyes darting about the kitchen and landing every-where but on him.

"I'll remember that and periodically drop a few crumbs for him to pick up. We want him to feel he's earning his keep, don't we?" Kin chuckled. "Well, shall we leave him to hold down the fort and head for the lodge for a few crumbs of our own?"

"Sure, if you really want to. But I'd be happy to make something here if you'd rather stay home."

"It's been a long day for both of us. Let's leave your vicious mutt here as a guard while we let Elly wait on us."

Conversations were suspended, and the clatter of cutlery on plates ceased, when they entered the lodge a short time later. A feeling of puzzlement crept over Amanda when she noticed a young couple trying to quiet their fussy infant even while they watched her and Kin. A pair of starry-eyed teenagers she recog-nized from school appeared to have lost interest in the chocolate soda they shared, and also watched her and Kin with wide eyes. She tripped when Kin stopped dead in his tracks in front of her, his eyes locking defensively with those of an ancient Athabascan man across the room.

Unblinking, Amanda, too, met the gaze of the old man as his eyes traveled over her critically. He was somebody important. She sensed it immediately from the sudden tension in the dining room. Long gray hair reached to the middle of his back in a loose braid and his weather-beaten face was a mass of wrinkles, reminding Amanda of a Shar-Pei dog she'd had as a child. His bony hands shook with the common ailment of the elderly as he raised a glass of water to his lips, meeting Kin's gaze with a look of censure. She wondered why he would be looking at her and Kin with such displeasure. Obviously, he had some grievance with Kin.

The man seated across the table was also an Athabascan who was a few decades younger. He smiled at Kin and Amanda and spoke quietly to the old man in the Athabascan language.

Lightly stomping his snow-covered boots on the rug at the door, Kin held Amanda's hand and led her across the room to the table occupied by the two men. Other diners continued watching with rapt attention and Amanda wondered wildly what kind of drama she had inadvertently walked in on.

Kin stopped at the table. "Chief Chena, this is Amanda Roberts, the new teacher. Mandy, this is Chief Chena and his son, Charles, er, Russell."

Russell! Amanda's brain screamed the name, and she smiled weakly at the two men. Her eyes flew to Kin, who was watching the old man defiantly. *Kin's father and grandfather. Kin is the grandson of the tribe's chief. Why didn't he tell me something so important? Why all the secrecy?*

Charles Russell held out a hand to Amanda, which she gratefully accepted after pulling off one mitten. When she turned to Chief Chena and her proffered hand was ignored with a stony look, her smile faded.

"Miss Roberts, Kincaid has told us of you. I suspect he has not paid you the same courtesy concerning us," the chief said in a reedy voice.

"Well, no, not exactly. I mean, he spoke of the chief and mentioned family, but didn't tell me they were one and the same." She forced a light laugh to which the chief did not respond.

Why do I feel as if I could cut the air with a knife? Her mind raced desperately in all directions. *Oh my gosh! I'm with Kin and they might expect him to be with Lucinda. Uh-oh!*

"He, uh, never mentioned he was in line to one day be chief." Why wouldn't he mention a matter that must give him great pride? A questioning glance at Kin's defensive profile gained her a mere squeeze of the hand.

Sorrow dripped from Chief Chena's next words. "It is possible Kincaid may never be chief. His priorities are not often what they should be."

"I'm sure Mandy is as hungry as I am," Kin said quickly. "It was nice seeing you, Grandfather, Father." He nodded politely, but his considerate words were unconvincing after the tense scene that had just unfolded.

They made their way to a table in the corner of the dining room, which, unlike the others in the room, had been covered with a red-and-white checked tablecloth and was graced by a candle. Amanda presumed Kin had called Elly and instructed her to provide a romantic setting. She felt a moment's pleasure when she looked into his emotion-filled eyes. They sat in silence for a while, making a pretense of studying their menus.

Finally, she couldn't keep quiet any longer. "Kin—"

"Mandy, I'm really sorry about that. I know you're

confused about what happened over there.'' He put down his menu and gazed at her earnestly. ''There's tension between Grandfather and me right now. But he was rude to you and there's no excuse for that. As chief, it's his duty to welcome you to Chena. He's got a problem with me right now and he took it out on you. Please accept my apology on his behalf.''

Amanda had the distinct impression he was skirting the issue. And she didn't intend to let him off the hook that easily. Her hands twisted in her lap before she plunged into waters where she knew she might not be welcome. ''He seemed to dislike me before he saw me. Why would he feel that way? He can't have been told I'm a bad teacher after only one week.''

Kin's smile was kind. ''He doesn't dislike you, and his attitude has nothing at all to do with your teaching. Actually, word is already out that you're an excellent teacher and very patient with the students.'' His smile broadened into a devilish grin. ''It was news to me to hear that you're *patient*.''

An obstinate look settled over her features, and she looked him in the eye. ''Don't try to change the subject. I want to know why I felt as if I was caught between the Hatfields and the McCoys over there.''

''Yep. Plainspoken, too,'' Kin quipped. The warning glint in her eye caused him to look sheepish, and he rubbed his chin thoughtfully before attempting to explain further. ''Grandfather is wary of cheechakos. He's seen so many come and go. He doesn't trust them to stick around and fulfill their obligations. We lose teachers from Outside all the time. If he had his way, only Alaska Natives would be hired here. Village life isn't so foreign to them.'' He leaned back in his seat and ran a hand through his hair. "He doesn't recognize that the influence from Outside only broadens kids' education."

"He sounds like someone else I know. And you're pretty open-minded all of a sudden. But he was more than wary. He resents me. I think you're lying like a rug."

She was surprised when Kin's hand reached across the table to grab hers. He held it firmly, in view of the entire dining room.

His eyes caressed her with their warmth. "Please don't be upset. He doesn't mean to be unkind, but just worries about the tribe."

"You're talking in riddles. I wouldn't hurt your tribe."

"Of course you wouldn't." His thumb stroked the back of her hand. "Do you want to stay here? Would you rather go home for dinner?"

With an eager nod, Amanda concurred. "Yeah, let's. I feel like we're under a microscope here."

Kin let go of her hand, and they stood to bundle up before going back outside. Without a backward glance for his father and grandfather, he led her out of the lodge.

Amanda babbled nervously as they settled into the vehicle. "If we go to your house, they'll show up. Maybe we should go to my house. But if we go there, they'll see your car and know you're there as soon as they leave the lodge. Maybe you should leave me at my house and go home alone. But my car is there and I'll need it in the morning and—"

"Whoa!" He laughed. "Calm down. No need to run a verbal marathon. Nobody wants to cause a ruckus. Don't be afraid of Grandfather, Mandy. We're going home to have dinner in front of the fire, and talk.''

"Well . . . all right. But I don't like it.''

Back at Kin's house, they prepared sandwiches from leftover meatloaf in the roomy kitchen. Taking the food and some hot cider, they settled in front of the fireplace.

"I think I'd feel better if you'd tell me why your grandfather behaved as he did.'' Amanda took a bite from her sandwich and waited for him to open up.

Flickering firelight danced across Kin's brooding copper face as he stared into the fire. Fortifying himself with a sip of cider, he tried to explain.

"After my father, I'll be chief, as you guessed. Some tribes elect chiefs, but here it passes from father to son. Unless the people think an election is necessary, of course. Grandfather thinks I spend too much time on my business and not enough on tribal affairs. He resents anything that takes me away from tribal responsibilities.''

"He thinks I'm taking you away from your tribal work,'' she concluded. "But he's also worried about Lucinda, isn't he?''

Kin frowned and set his plate aside. "I don't know why you think Lucinda's involved. She's got nothing to do with it. She and Grandfather are close, but that's got nothing to do with my problems with him.''

Pleasant surprise surged momentarily through Amanda at his vehement denial of Lucinda's importance. Surely Elly was mistaken in her assumption that Kin and Lucinda were anything other than good friends. After all, they had grown up together. Maybe it was only natural for the maternal waitress to expect something special to come of their friendship.

Exasperation tightened Kin's voice when he continued, after another sip of drink. ''Anyway, nothing makes any sense because I'm doing my job.'' He stared silently into the fire for a moment, then went on. ''Years ago, I brought a woman here. She was from the Lower Forty-eight and I planned to marry her. I was young and in love and I neglected my duties. I concentrated only on my growing business and her. He remembers that time and forgets I'm older and more responsible now. He won't recognize that I know my priorities.''

Amanda felt the air rush from her lungs when he talked about the woman he'd planned to marry. She took a deep breath. ''What happened to the woman you were engaged to?''

He shook his head in remembrance. ''She hated it here and broke it off. It's just as well. Once I got over the pain and grew up a little, I realized it would never have worked. We had different wants and needs. I was in love with someone I'd created in my mind. The real thing was nothing like my fantasy.''

He picked up his sandwich and nibbled thoughtfully on a corner. ''I built this house for her, put my heart and soul into it. But she considered herself sophisticated, and liked everything modern and white and sterile-looking. Rustic wasn't her style. Chena—the bush—wasn't her style.''

There was no bitterness or melancholy in his words. He apparently cherished no sad feelings about losing the woman, although it explained why he believed she couldn't be trusted to stay in Chena. And his grandfather felt the same way.

"So your grandfather sort of expects me to be the same type of woman because I'm also from Outside?"

He tossed the remainder of his cider down his throat and poured more into both of their cups. "I guess that's about the size of it. And you rent one of my properties, so you're doubly guilty of distracting me as part of my business world."

A knot of disappointment formed in her stomach. So, that's what she was. Part of his business. Well, what could she expect? There were rumors, at least from Elly, that he was involved with Lucinda. And, though he'd mellowed a great deal, he had made it clear he didn't think Amanda belonged in the bush.

She'd kidded herself into thinking they were something other than mere friends, but he was only sowing his wild oats with an interesting newcomer. It was her own fault she'd allowed herself to be caught up in his game and had fallen in love. He'd made it clear from their first meeting on the bridge how he felt about cheechakos. She took another bite of her sandwich, which had suddenly lost its zest.

Kin's next words made her wonder if he was a mind reader. "It's just Grandfather who sees you as part of my business. I certainly don't."

Amanda's heart soared before she decided he was only being nice. He didn't see her as a business problem, but as a friend. It was that simple, and amounted to the same thing. He wasn't in love with her.

"Earth to Mandy."

She came out of her reverie with a thud. "Sorry. I

guess I'm tired after the adventure of the last two days.''

"You may as well go to bed early since tomorrow is a school day." He bit into his half-eaten sandwich.

They finished their meal in silence while the warm fire crackled nearby. Kin refused to allow Amanda to help clean the kitchen, insisting instead that she take a long, hot soak in the tub. He gave her fresh towels from the linen closet and wickedly told her he'd try to remember she was in the tub so he didn't ''accidentally'' barge in on her. Amanda gave him a saccharine smile and ostentatiously clicked the lock on the bathroom door. His hearty laugh echoed down the hall as he headed back to the kitchen.

After her bath, Amanda put on a flannel gown with long sleeves and a high, embroidered collar and shoved her feet into fuzzy slippers. She pulled on a robe before peeking out of the bathroom into the deserted hall.

An amused voice stopped her just as she reached the door of her room. "Is that sexy outfit for my benefit?"

She whirled around to find Kin strolling down the hall, a teasing light in his dark eyes. Her cheeks felt hot and she tugged self-consciously at the belt of the robe, realizing how silly she must look in her old-maidish getup. All it needed was a shower cap and face cream to complete the picture.

Kin leaned casually against the frame of her door. "You know, I just love well-wrapped packages. They usually contain the most charming things." His eyes danced as he reached out and tugged lightly at the little bow she had tied at the top of her high-necked gown.

Amanda's hand inadvertently went to the untied bow before she recovered and said lightly, "You're going to have to break this bad habit." She laughed with joy at the completely baffled look on Kin's face. "Catching me in my nightwear," she explained. "Is it a habit of long standing or am I just lucky to always have you show up when I'm dressed this way?"

Exuberant laughter burst forth from Kin. He was so ruggedly handsome, standing there with one long leg crossed casually in front of the other, arms folded over his rumbling chest. She itched to reach out and touch the weathered creases, made more prominent on his dark face by animation, and to push the glossy hair back out of his eyes as it slid forward in his mirth.

Kin's eyes darkened at the play of emotions across her face, and his own hand came up to tenderly stroke her rosy cheek. "Sweet dreams, Princess. My room is right next door if you need me for anything."

"Good night." She turned blindly to enter her room and close the door.

Unable to banish Kin from her thoughts, unwilling to forget the warmth of his lips every time they kissed, she lay awake for a long time. It was late when she finally heard him stirring in the next room and tried to visualize what he was doing, what each sound signified as he prepared for bed. Long after quiet had settled over the house, she tossed fitfully, still unable to sleep, overcome by thoughts of the man in the next room.

* * *

The insistent beeping of the alarm clock cut into Amanda's consciousness. It seemed only minutes since she had finally fallen asleep. Dressed in a black corduroy jumper over a red cowl-neck sweater, she groggily applied her usual minimal amount of makeup, and padded to the kitchen in fuzzy, hot-pink slippers. Kin was already there, drinking a cup of coffee, and she was perversely gratified to see that he appeared not to have slept well, either. A flicker of humor lit his drowsy eyes as his gaze fell on the bright pink slippers that clashed with the red pantyhose covering her legs.

He poured her a cup of coffee. "You look charming this morning, Mandy. I especially like the footwear. It goes so well with the rest of your outfit."

Amanda was not in the mood to talk, let alone exert her sense of humor. "*I* thought so," she replied crossly.

They sat down together at the kitchen table for a quiet breakfast of hot oatmeal, which Kin had just prepared. When they were nearly finished, Amanda roused herself just enough to venture a question.

"Who do I call to fix my pipes?"

"I'll take care of that. I have to call a man in Tok and see if he can come out here today. You'd better wake up before you leave for school." He poured her another cup of coffee as she stifled a yawn.

"I'm not a morning person," she mumbled dully.

He grinned and leaned forward, causing her frown to deepen as he scrutinized her face. "Could have fooled me. I've seen you up early a few times and you've always been a live wire. Is it possible you didn't sleep very well?"

"Guess not." The short reply and a dark look dared him to delve into the reason for her insomnia.

He ignored narrowed eyes, stood, and rubbed her drooping shoulders. "I wonder why. Well, I'll do whatever I can to make sure you sleep like a baby tonight. You need to relax to begin with."

His touch awakened her in record time. She fidgeted, crossing and uncrossing her feet and twisting her napkin, shoulders burning where he rubbed them with gentle hands.

"What makes you think I'll be here tonight? If the man from Tok fixes my pipes, I'll go back home." The no-nonsense tone after previous sleepy grumblings caused him to blink in surprise.

"It's not always easy to fix frozen pipes, Mandy. And I'd like you to think of this house as your home, at least until everything is fixed at the A-frame."

His hand on her shoulder was really beginning to play havoc with her senses. She stood and picked up the empty cereal bowls to take them to the sink, feeling his eyes on her as she rinsed the dishes and put them in the dishwasher. She filled Frosty's food bowl and placed it on the floor, then turned to face Kin, shifting uneasily under the intensity of his gaze.

"Do I have a run in my stocking or something?"

"Personally, I can't find a thing wrong with how you look. Except possibly your neon footwear."

"Yes, well, I guess I'd better do something about that." She headed toward the kitchen door but stopped when he rose from the table to stand in front of her.

"If you'll give me your car keys, I'll start your car so it can warm up. I plugged it in last night so you won't have any problems. But you don't have to leave right away.'' He stood very close and his simple offer hinted that he'd like to spend some time with her while the car warmed up.

"M-my keys. I'll get them. Thank you." She inched past him and headed quickly down the hall, muttering under her breath as she entered her room.

"Why does he have to be so gorgeous? Even after a night when he obviously didn't sleep any better than I did. Gee!" It must be possible to literally drown in his eyes. And if not, his heady kisses would surely melt her very bones.

"Every time he kisses me, I feel like a puddle of mush." Continuing to grumble, she searched first her purse and then her coat pocket for the keys. "This is exquisite torture." Finding the keys in a pocket, she turned to take them to Kin and almost ran into him in the middle of the bedroom.

Chapter Eight

Amanda's breathing seemed to stop while she frantically tried to recall if she had muttered loudly or clearly enough for him to understand. "I, uh, didn't know you were in here. I mean, uh, that you followed me," she stammered.

"Obviously." His low tone made it clear he had heard and understood plenty. He raised a finger to trace along her jaw and down the side of her neck.

She held out the car keys, her quickening pulse causing her hand to shake. "Yes, well, here are the keys."

Kin's voice was smooth and insistent. He took the keys from her and tossed them on a chair. "Let Hailey play with the keys."

They breathed in unison as he pulled her against him, enfolding her in his arms. Their lips touched and she stroked his thick black hair, pulling his face closer. His mouth moved to her flushed cheeks and throat with kisses, before he lay his cheek against hers.

She touched his dark head with loving hands. "Oh, Kin, I . . ." Should she admit she loved him? She wanted to burst with the happy news, but his simply being nice to her didn't mean he returned the feeling. Kidding herself that his improved attitude toward her constituted love wouldn't make it real.

Kin buried his face in the perfumed curve of her neck. "Yes, sweetheart?"

Breathlessly, she said the first thing that came to mind, stroking one hand down his smooth black hair. "I . . . I have to go to work."

Releasing a ragged breath, his gaze wandered first to her mouth, then her eyes. A slow, devastating smile creased his features. "Consider this a temporary reprieve. I intend to exert all my efforts to make this short encounter a mere prelude to a much more serious one later on." He stole one more short kiss before releasing her.

Arriving at the school a short time later, she met Pete Smith on the porch, tacking a sign on the locked door. Due to frozen pipes, the school would be closed for several days.

"The pipes froze and broke in several places." Picking up his briefcase, he joined her on the walk back to her car. "I'll let you know when we're ready to reopen. This has happened before, though not for many years. Precautions sometimes just aren't enough if it gets far enough below zero."

They arrived at her car and Amanda turned to him

with one hand on the door. "What about the kids? Will they start showing up?"

"Chena has a high-tech grapevine, so I'm not worried about that. And I've called all the teachers. You were the only one I couldn't reach. Guess I called just as you left home."

A sudden fit of coughing seized Amanda as her breath caught in her throat. Pete didn't know she had spent the night at Kin's house.

"Uh, yes, you must have," she wheezed.

"Speaking of grapevines, I hear you and Kin took a sled ride this weekend."

"He came up with a unique way of taking me to Tok," she admitted when she had regained her breath and thought of some response. Was Pete about to censure her for the trip? He must have heard it was an overnight trip. She rushed on in an effort to dispel any wrong ideas he might have. "It was actually quite unexpected. For me, I mean. I never expected to ride a dogsled when I came to Alaska. Except for sport, I thought they were a thing of the past."

"It's true that even above the Arctic Circle, snowmobiles have replaced sleds. But it's an extremely popular sport, and Kin's a top-notch musher. He wins a lot of races. I'm glad you two had a good time. Kin's been pretty preoccupied lately and it's good to know he's relaxing."

He headed for his car and then turned back to her. "You hurry home and take something for that cough. Don't want our new teacher laid up with a bad cold. Might give our temperate climate a bad name." With a chuckle at his own humor, he waved and continued toward his car.

Amanda nearly choked on his well-meant advice. Kicking the snow off her mukluks, she returned the wave and got into her car. Was it possible there was no substance to Elly's idea about a romance between Lucinda and Kin? Surely if it were true, Lucinda's own father would know about it. But he didn't act the least bothered that Kin had taken Amanda on an overnight trip, so maybe it was just a product of Elly's imagination.

Even Kin himself acted like he wasn't aware of the supposed relationship. Of course, even if Lucinda weren't in the picture, it didn't help Amanda. He still had a prejudice against cheechakos.

She drove the three miles back to her own house, not yet ready to face Kin after their recent encounter. He had only to look at her to send her senses spinning out of control and she needed to be alone for a while to get a grip on her emotions before seeing him again.

Kin had said somebody would have to come from Tok to repair her pipes. It was still early, so she decided to hang around the house for a while. Maybe a plumber would show up and fix everything and then she'd have to return to Kin's house for the sole purpose of collecting her belongings and Frosty.

She changed into jeans before starting a roaring fire in the Franklin stove. After going upstairs to wash her hands, she selected a new mystery novel from the bookcase and went back downstairs to curl up on the couch.

But she was unable to concentrate on her book, her mind heavily occupied instead by Kin's strange insistence on bringing her into his home while her pipes were frozen. That was going far beyond the call of duty for a landlord.

Something about those frozen pipes bothered her. Her hands thumbed unconsciously through the pages of the paperback novel and suddenly Lucinda and Kin flew from her mind. Her hands. She had *washed* her hands right here in a house with frozen pipes. How could that be?

She ran back upstairs and turned on the water in both the sink and tub, even flushing the toilet. Everything worked perfectly. Racing headlong down the stairs, she tried the same thing in the lower bathroom, again meeting with success. But when she went to the kitchen and turned the faucet on and off, nothing happened.

A perplexed frown settled over her face as she sat on the floor and leaned against the refrigerator, staring at the dry sink. She was no plumber, but this didn't make sense. Could it be that certain pipes had not frozen? Possibly. If that were the case, she'd tell Kin she would live in her own house and use the water from the bathroom until the kitchen pipes were fixed.

Of course, Kin had mentioned the possibility of flooding. She wouldn't want to be there if that happened. Odd that he hadn't shown any concern about removing the furniture, *his* furniture, since it would be damaged in a flood. Come to think of it, he had been awfully casual about the idea of the destruction that could result from a flood. Almost as if it wasn't really a possibility.

A sudden, unpleasant suspicion gnawed at the back of her mind as she stared at the dry faucet. Surely, he wouldn't . . . Slowly, she knelt on the kitchen floor and opened the cabinet under the sink. She hesitated, chewing thoughtfully on her bottom lip before turning the faucet handles under the sink. Water gushed into the sink where she had left the faucet turned on. She sat back on her haunches and watched the water run freely.

Kin must have turned off the faucet under the sink. He had turned off the water in the kitchen and told her she had to move out of her house, practically forcing her to move into his own home. Why was he so adamant that she not stay at the lodge, but with him instead?

The embrace they had shared that morning sprang to mind, momentarily betraying her building outrage at what he had done. Would he play such an elaborate trick just to romance her? If not, just what was he up to?

There was only one way to find out. Turning off the faucet, she rushed to get her coat from the closet. She spared only a moment's thought about the fire in the Franklin stove. It was well screened and she didn't anticipate being gone long. She'd soon be home with her suitcase and her dog, whether Kincaid Russell liked it or not.

When she pulled up in front of Kin's house, he walked out on the front porch to meet her. A glimpse at the stormy look on her face as she marched up to the porch caused his bright smile to dim somewhat.

"I just came from my house, *where I washed my hands in the sink,*" she said stonily. "I thought you might be the person to tell me how I was able to do that. While you're at it, you might tell me again just exactly why I'm staying here with you. You can explain these things while I pack.'' She stalked past him into the house and headed for her room.

Kin raised his eyes heavenward and followed her. ''Mandy, I had to do what I did. Before you pack, I think you should listen to what I'd hoped not to have to tell you. I have a good reason for wanting you to stay here with me.''

Shaking her head, Amanda turned on him, hands planted firmly on her hips. ''It's obvious you want me here, but I'd like to hear more about your so-called 'good reason.' I just can't believe the lengths you went to in order to get me here. You actually turned off the kitchen water to convince me my pipes were frozen. I absolutely cannot believe you did that. Why did you do that?'' Her voice rose an octave and she threw her hands out in supplication. ''What is so doggone important about getting me to stay here with you?''

Kin took a deep breath, appearing to consider exactly what he should tell her, but the set look on her face must have convinced him of the necessity for plain speaking. Silently, he reached into his back pocket and extracted his wallet. Opening it, he took out a small plastic bag containing a scrap of paper, which he handed to her.

'' 'Curiosity killed the cat,' '' Amanda read aloud. She rolled her eyes and went on sarcastically, ''Oh, well that explains everything. Now it's as clear as mud. Kin, what is going on? I want to know *now*. What does this paper have to do with me?''

He looked at her gravely. ''Yesterday when we arrived at your house, I found this sitting on your kitchen counter. Is it yours?''

"No."

"Do you know whose it is?"

"No."

"Do you know how it got there?"

"No."

"Well, I want to know." A hard look entered his eyes. "I already have some suspicions. Mandy, do you remember the argument we had last week about your watching airplanes landing late at night?"

She looked incredulous, wondering how he could think she'd forget it. "Of course. You were so ridiculous, I doubt I'll ever forget it. But what has that got to do with the price of tea in China?" She tapped a foot in double time while awaiting his answer.

His smile was grim. He took the note from her as she turned and pulled her suitcase out of the closet to begin packing.

"I was upset about you watching those planes because I believe they're smugglers' planes. I don't want you involved in something dangerous." He put the note back into his wallet and returned it to his back pocket, going to sit on the end of the bed.

The ominous words made Amanda stop in the middle of the room with a handful of lingerie. She eyed him curiously. *Now* what game was he playing?

"This note makes me think you might have been seen watching those planes," he continued. "I think someone got into your house while we were out of town and left this note as a warning to mind your own business."

Chills raced up her spine and she gaped at him in disbelief. Smugglers? Cryptic warnings? Breaking and entering? In Chena? He must be mistaken. She

looked him doubtfully in the eye but saw no subter-
fuge, no games, and definitely no humor. The man
was actually serious.

She made her way to a rocking chair by the window and sat tensely on the edge, still gripping the
handful of clothes. "You're not kidding. You really
believe someone broke into my house because I
watched some silly airplanes landing at night," she
said, almost in a whisper.

Kin faced her from where he sat on the edge of the
bed. "That's why I wanted you here. This is a tiny
village, and everyone knows who you are and where
you live. The smugglers know who to go after," he
said in a desperate tone. "I can't ensure your safety
if you stay at the A-frame or at the lodge. You'd be
all alone at night. If someone wanted to harm you
because of something you've seen, you could be in
real danger."

Disbelief washed over Amanda, causing her to
slide deeper into the rocker. "But this is ridiculous,"
she sputtered. "What makes you think people would
want to smuggle things into Chena? And what on
earth would they smuggle here? Drugs?"

"Liquor."

Amanda grinned at the ridiculous assertion.
"Booze? Why? Prohibition ended a long time ago.
Word is out that you no longer have to smuggle it."

"Mandy, you know booze can't be bought in
Chena, except in my bar, one night a week, by the
glass. Chief Chena wanted to make the village completely dry like many other villages, but some residents raised a fuss."

"Okay, but all anyone has to do is drive to Tok

and stock up on booze for their home," she countered, unclear as to why there should be a smuggling problem just because of a tribal rule.

"The main reason for not going totally dry is because we're near the Alcan and it might be a little extra revenue from tourists. That makes no sense because we're off the main road and tourists aren't going to come here just for a drink."

"But why would anyone smuggle from Canada when booze is so much cheaper in this country, anyway?"

Heaving a frustrated sigh, Kin shook his head. "We don't know where it's coming from. Could be Anchorage or Fairbanks. It's still smuggling, though, because they sneak it into town at night in violation of local regulations, and then probably sell it here. We also think they're trucking or flying the goods to other bush villages after leaving some here with locals," he told her. "They'd make a neat profit in dry villages all over the state. And believe it or not, a lot of locals never go to Tok. So if they want booze, dealing with a smuggler is easiest."

Amanda found it quite a challenge to digest all this. In her mind was a Pollyanna vision of Chena as a happy little village in a safe, remote location. Kin's claims poked holes in her fantasy and left her feeling rather foolish.

"Can't the police do something? If you're so sure about all this, why don't they just stop the smugglers? And they could arrest the locals who are involved."

Shaking his head again, Kin explained. "Paul Donaldson is trying to help, but you have to understand that this is a violation of Chena tribal law. It's not a violation of any law the troopers can enforce. Paul is helping as a friend, not in his official capacity as a trooper. However, if you are being threatened, it becomes of interest to the police.''

A light bulb went on inside Amanda's head. ''I guess that explains some of his questions to me. He was trying to find out if I'd noticed anything besides the planes.''

''We need to catch them in the act or with the goods. You unwittingly helped by telling both of us about the late-night flights, since yours is the only house in town near the airfield.'' Kin ran a hand through his glossy hair in frustration, stood and went to gaze out the window. ''But they never come when we're watching for them. It's like they have no set schedule, so we never know when they'll show up.''

Amanda got up to go put the lingerie in her suitcase, then walked to the closet to remove clothes. ''Why did you turn off my water and lie to me? Why didn't you show me the note and tell me the truth? Nothing you're saying seems to tie in with that.''

Kin turned back to face her. ''Mandy, I wish you wouldn't do that.''

She tossed some clothes into the bag before going to take more personal items out of a dresser drawer. ''Do what? Pack my things so I can go home? I really think it's best,'' she said in a carefully controlled voice. There would be time later to deal with the horrible, heavy weight that had settled on her heart.

A deep crease marred his weathered forehead as he watched her pack. ''I didn't want you involved. You would have been if I'd told you anything. Of course, this note proves they already know you're on to them, even though you didn't know it yourself. It also proves they might feel compelled to do something about you.''

''Then I won't tell them I know anything.'' She flicked her wrist airily. This wasn't the time to tell Kin about the man who had watched her through the window of the pickup. ''I'm not a total fool, you know.''

With a wan smile, Kin acknowledged this. ''You're not a fool at all, Mandy—''

''Kincaid Russell saying I'm not a fool? Can I get that in writing? And I want three people to witness your signature,'' she interrupted with great spirit. It appeared she had made progress in her mission to prove to him that she wasn't some helpless city slicker on a vacation in the bush.

Though he ignored her request, Kin's grimace told her she had hit her mark. ''That's why I know you'll understand and accept my explanation,'' he continued. ''When I saw the note on the counter, I had to decide quickly what to do. I decided to keep you in the dark, protecting you by getting you out of the house. They'd obviously gotten in to leave the note there, and that scared the heck out of me.''

''But how long did you expect to get away with it? You knew I planned to have the pipes fixed by tomorrow at the latest.''

Kin scuffed the toe of his boot on the carpet and avoided her eyes. ''I was going to go to the house today and turn off all the other faucets as a precaution against your discovering the truth. Then I was going to tell you the plumber in Tok was swamped and didn't know when he could get here. Meanwhile, you'd live here, where I could ensure your safety.''

There was no apology in his tone for the web of lies he'd created to protect her.

He looked at her curiously. "What are you doing here, anyway? Why aren't you at work?''

The irony that had led to the discovery that her pipes weren't frozen struck Amanda and she laughed, albeit with little mirth. "The pipes at the school really are frozen. Some of them even burst. Pete said the school will be closed for a while.''

Kin's jaw dropped. "If I didn't know better, I'd take that personally as a trick of fate.'' He shook his head in amazement. "I lie about your pipes being frozen and a real set of frozen pipes proves my undoing.''

"No. Only the undoing of your lie," she said in a level tone.

He ignored the jab and held her gaze, his voice quiet. "Will you reconsider and stay here now? I'd like to call Paul and arrange to plant someone inside the A-frame at night.'' He tapped a finger thoughtfully against his chin. "If word gets around that you're not staying there, and nobody sees any lights on or smoke coming from the chimney, the smugglers might become less cautious and we might catch them. But it may take a few days.''

Amanda considered his plan. "Had you intended to plant someone in my house anyway, while I stayed here? Without telling me about this?''

Kin flushed and his eyes left hers. "Yes.''

"You really have some colossal nerve," she snapped. The chair she had occupied before looked inviting all of a sudden and she walked over and sat down hard, feeling oddly dejected. "You were going to lead me along by the nose, making sure I never knew a thing, even though my home was to be used for a stakeout in my absence. You should join the feds. They love this cloak-and-dagger stuff," she said bitterly.

What upset her the most was the knowledge that everything he had done was due to his belief that she was some weak, helpless female. Nothing had changed, not really. He was treating her just like Dad did.

Feeling restless, she arose again and went to stand by the window, reflecting in silence on the sadness seeping through her. Kin had only wanted her at his house so he could use the A-frame for a secret stakeout. He was concerned for her safety because he had no faith in her. It was common decency to remove someone from known danger, but the person in danger should at least be told what was going on. His heart wasn't even involved. It was his feeling of superiority that dictated his thoughts and actions.

"Will you agree to it?" he asked when she turned to face him.

She was trying to get a grip on her emotions and he had to bother her with riddles. "Agree to what?"

"Agree to what we've been discussing. Agree to stay here and let us use your house for the, er, stakeout, as you put it?"

Suddenly, it was all too much. She just couldn't care about smugglers and notes and stakeouts when what she really wanted to do was crawl into a corner and nurse the anguish of a lost dream. A lost dream of love. She waved a careless hand at him. "Sure. I don't care. But please do it quickly so I can go back home as soon as possible." Something resembling pain flashed in Kin's eyes as she shrugged out of her coat, but a closer look told her she must have been mistaken, for his features appeared rather blank.

Then she remembered something he had said a few minutes earlier. "There's smoke coming from my chimney right now. I went home after leaving the school and started a fire. That's when I washed my hands and found out the pipes weren't frozen. I just came back here to give you a piece of my mind and get my things."

Ready to take action, Kin spoke over his shoulder on his way to the door. "We may as well go over and put out the fire. The sooner the place starts to look unoccupied, the sooner we can catch these guys. And we need to meet with Paul to discuss the plan."

Within the hour they had smothered the fire in Amanda's woodstove and returned to Kin's house to work out a plan of action with Paul, who was as disturbed by the cryptic note as Kin had been. Amanda spoke little during the meeting, since they would do things their own way, regardless of any input from her. She silently cursed the smugglers for causing all of this, leading her to mistakenly believe Kin's concern for her arose from anything other than civic duty.

Kin left when Paul did, saying he'd be working at the store and lodge, casually spreading the word that the A-frame was empty for a while, due to frozen pipes. Amanda wondered if he was also going to tell the whole village where she was staying while she was out of her home. That little tidbit of information ought to keep village tongues wagging.

When a knock sounded on the front door a short time later, she grasped the barking Frosty by his new collar and opened the door to find Lucinda Smith standing on the porch, bundled in her expensive fur parka. As always, Amanda was struck by her cool beauty and wondered how she could have thought to compete with such a striking woman for the interest of Kincaid Russell.

"Hello, Amanda," Lucinda said with a bright smile. "I'd heard you were living here."

Offering the woman her own somewhat pensive smile, Amanda stepped back to allow her into the warmth of the house. "Well, I wouldn't say I'm *living* here, exactly," she began. She bit her lip as the thought occurred to her that she had done nothing at all to be ashamed of. Pushing the door closed, she let go of Frosty's collar so he could sniff the newcomer's mukluks, and went on in a firmer voice. "Kin has kindly given me a haven until my frozen pipes are fixed."

Although she and Kin hadn't discussed it, she assumed he wanted her to stick to the cover story with everybody. If he wanted to tell Lucinda or anybody else the truth, that was up to him. She helped the other woman out of her coat and hung it in the hall closet before leading her to the living room.

Making herself comfortable on the couch, Lucinda looked up at Amanda. "Is Kin around? There's something I need to discuss with him."

Amanda shook her head. "He left a couple of hours ago and hasn't returned. You might find him at the lodge or the store," she suggested helpfully. "Or if you'd like to wait, can I make you some coffee or tea?"

Lucinda smiled. "Tea would be nice. I believe Kin keeps some cranberry spice herbal tea on hand. It's a favorite of mine."

Happy to be able to escape her visitor's company for a few minutes, Amanda planted a smile on her face, said, "Back in a minute," and headed for the kitchen, the contents of which Lucinda appeared to possess an intimate knowledge of. That thought brought her no comfort in regards to her concern about a possible romantic relationship between two old friends. Maybe Elly was right, after all.

The tea was ready all too soon and she was forced to return to the living room, where Lucinda was looking at a magazine from the coffee table. To her dismay, the woman set aside the magazine and appeared ready for a chat. But she was soon surprised at how easily they conversed, and it again occurred to her that Elly might be mistaken about a romance between her landlord and this charming woman. This inability to decide whether or not Elly knew what she was talking about was getting irritating.

They were finishing their second cup of tea when the front door slammed and Kin's warm, deep voice greeted Frosty before he entered the living room. Amanda disappeared back into the kitchen, giving them privacy for their talk. She didn't want to inadvertently eavesdrop, so she looked around for a radio to drown out the voices. Remembering there was no radio reception in Chena, she forced herself to concentrate on watching some chickadees nipping at the suet Kin had tied to a tree for them outside the kitchen window.

When the voices in the living room retreated down the hall, a large knot formed in the pit of her stomach. She rearranged the salt and pepper shakers on the table several times and then squeezed her eyes tightly shut when tears blurred her view of the birds. The den lay down that hall, and there were all kinds of reasons Kin and Lucinda might go there. Anyway, what did it matter to her where they went or what they did?

Squaring her shoulders, she went into the living room, making herself comfortable in a high-backed chair that faced the fireplace. She tried to read a mystery she had left there earlier in the day, but this just wasn't the day for concentration. Her mind wandered curiously down the hall despite her valiant efforts to restrain it. Then she heard Kin and Lucinda coming back, speaking in warm, quiet tones. They went to the hall closet, where Kin helped Lucinda with her parka.

"The ring is beautiful," she heard Lucinda say with a catch in her voice. "I only want you to be happy. You know that."

Kin's deep voice carried into the living room. "And that's what I want for you."

Lucinda left the house and Amanda renewed her determination to try to concentrate on the book in which she had not turned a page. She tried desperately to shut out of her mind Lucinda's words about a beautiful ring, but they seemed to be suspended in neon lights in the air above her book. Kin approached her chair and stood looking down at her.

She lifted her eyes and met his gaze with an innocent expression. "Did Lucinda leave already?"

The corners of his mouth twitched with amusement. "Yes, Lucinda left already." He directed a knowing look at her. "You must be reading a good book, not to have heard her go."

"Can't put it down," she lied.

He squatted on the stone hearth in front of her. "I see. I understand you two had a nice visit. I'm glad. I want very much for you to be friends." He picked up a poker to rearrange the burning logs in the fireplace.

While she watched him stoke the fire, Amanda considered her next words carefully. "Look, I don't want to be the cause of trouble. I would be happy to stay in Tok and commute during this smuggling thing. Just say the word and I'm out of here." It pained her to say it, but it was the only decent thing to do.

Kin set the poker aside, confusion in his eyes. "Everything is fine. By the way, I told Lucy what's really going on. We've been very close all our lives and there's no problem with her knowing the truth. Our only problem is the smugglers."

Amanda watched the firelight reflect in a bluish sheen on his black hair, and thought that dark blue color reflected her mood right about now. Though not feeling any of the generosity of spirit she displayed, she persisted. "Still, it might be better for me to move to Tok for the duration of the stakeout."

Annoyance registered on Kin's face. "Mandy, the only issue here is your safety. I live in this big house alone. There's plenty of room and nobody is going to be bothered by your staying here. Case closed."

He stood and stretched his long, denim-clad legs and Amanda noticed he was wearing cowboy boots, which only served to accent his lean form. She raised an eyebrow. "Pretty impractical footwear for this weather, don't you think?"

There was an invitation in the depths of his eyes. "I'm in the mood to live dangerously." He reached down and took the book, placing it on the arm of the chair. Taking her hands in his, he pulled her to her feet and against his chest in one fluid movement. His arms cuddled her in a snug cocoon while she stroked the solid muscles of his broad back.

Oh, so softly, he caressed her flushed cheek with his thumb and feathered kisses over her eyes. The fire seemed to leave the confines of the fireplace and engulf her, melting her knees and weakening her spirit to fight her love for him. She sighed in his warm embrace before an object, small and hard, pressed against her breastbone, causing her to wince. She pulled away a little and glanced down at his front shirt pocket. Something was there, something small and blockish, like a box . . . a ring box . . .

The jangling seemed to come from far away at first. Then gradually, it became an irritant, repeating itself until Kin, unaware of Amanda's painful diversion, set her away from himself to answer the telephone. Whoever was on the other end grabbed his attention immediately, and he sat on the edge of the couch to listen, an intent look on his face.

It took great effort for Amanda not to stare at his bulging shirt pocket. Forcing herself to look anywhere but at Kin, Amanda's gaze fell on a collection of framed photos sitting on the fireplace mantel alongside various pieces of Alaskan Native art. One of the pictures was of a slightly younger Kin and Lucinda, their arms around each other and their legs tied together for a three-legged race. The picture couldn't have been taken more than five years ago.

Her eyes moved to the large picture window displaying the white wonderland outside and Lucinda's private words to Kin echoed through her mind. *"The ring is beautiful . . . I only want you to be happy."* A kick in the stomach couldn't have taken her breath away more quickly. How on earth could she have forgotten?

What was the story about the ring Lucinda had mentioned? Kin had made it pretty obvious he had some feelings for Amanda. Would he be giving Lucinda a friendship ring at his age? Unlikely. And he certainly wouldn't be kissing Amanda mere minutes after giving the other woman an engagement ring. Maybe it was an old family heirloom he'd showed Lucinda. But why?

Kin hung up the phone and turned to her, a grim look on his face. "That was Paul. Seems there's been some sabotage to my planes. Joseph found it when he was checking the tie-downs."

"Joseph works for you?"

"I find things to keep him busy so he can earn money." Kin gazed out the window with a frown. "Nobody but the smugglers would have done this. But why would they fool with my planes?"

Amanda shrugged helplessly. "Have you ever used your planes in an attempt to track them or anything?"

"No. I've never gotten that close." He rubbed the

back of his neck and continued to gaze at the pristine world beyond the window.

Considering his words, she looked at him keenly. "Or have you?"

She had his attention now, and he turned to face her with a frown. "What do you mean?"

"Maybe you've been closer than you thought. Maybe you've made them nervous by something you've done, and they're trying to be sure you *can't* use your planes for some reason."

Something flashed in his eyes and he headed out of the living room to the coat closet. Grabbing his mukluks, he sat on a bench and pulled off the cowboy boots.

"I just wish I had an inkling of what they think I know." He rolled his eyes in frustration and tugged at the laces of the fur boots. "Mandy, I've got to get over to the field to see what can be done about the damage."

He stood and shrugged into his parka, then pulled a pair of warm gloves out of one pocket before turning to place his hands on her shoulders. "But you and I have some unfinished business to attend to when I get back, so don't disappear."

Her heart fluttered at the warm look in his eyes and she managed a wavering smile. "I'll look forward to it. While you're gone, I think I'll take Frosty for a walk."

"Don't stray far." He looked intently into her eyes and tucked a strand of hair behind her ear. "I don't want to misplace you."

"Uh . . . we'll only go to the end of the road, since I've never been that far." With an effort, she broke eye contact and controlled her unsteady voice. Her trembling fingers reached to fumble with the zipper on his parka. "You'd better zip up. It's cold out there."

Snatching the zipper, he pulled it up, then enfolded her in his arms. "Seems a crime to go out there when it's so warm in here." His lips brushed hers in a tantalizing caress.

"I've been meaning to turn down that thermostat," she murmured against his lips, deliberately misunderstanding him. "Now, you'd better get going or else you'll still be out there after dark." She gave him a little push toward the door.

Kin's Blazer was soon headed around the bend toward the airfield, and Amanda went to her room to prepare for a walk with Frosty. She toyed with the idea of putting on long underwear, then cast it aside in the confident knowledge that they wouldn't be gone long. In no time, she was headed along the frozen road at a brisk pace, going in the opposite direction from the village center, the fluorescent mutt running in circles ahead of her.

Chapter Nine

Paying no attention to where she was going, Amanda followed Frosty on his merry dance along the road leading away from Kin's house, away from Kin. After a while, the road came to an abrupt end and a trail led off into the frozen muskeg among the spindly black spruce. Frosty earned a wan smile from her as he wriggled from end to end in anticipation of a longer walk.

"Want to go exploring?" It wouldn't hurt to follow the trail for a short distance.

The trail was made by snowmobiles. Amanda had learned to recognize the tracks of the popular sport-and-utility vehicles during her short time in Chena.

She was surprised when a rickety plywood structure built on the edge of a clearing loomed up ahead. There were no windows and no sign of life as Amanda moved forward curiously. It didn't appear to

154

be anyone's home. When she rounded the corner of the building, there was a door with two snowmobiles parked nearby. Not wanting to be accused of trespassing or snooping, she started back toward the road.

Hearing the door open, she turned to explain her presence and recognized Kirk, one of the men who had helped her move into the A-frame. Then she was suddenly grabbed from behind, and a hand clapped over her mouth. She struggled and squirmed, kicking at the man who held her, and at Kirk, in front. She had a vague awareness of Frosty growling and barking somewhere nearby.

When somebody else stepped out of the shack, she froze in shock. It was the bearded man she had gazed down upon in the pickup truck that night from her bedroom window. *Oh, no . . .* Amanda closed her eyes, shook her head, and reopened them, only to find the menacing fellow standing in front of her. His eyes were hard as nails, and he watched Amanda with contempt. At his brief nod to the man who held her, the hand was removed from over her mouth, although she was still held in a strong grip.

"Oh, no . . ."

"Oh, yes, little Miss Tenderfoot. You snooped beyond your safety zone this time," the man sneered. "Why couldn't you just mind your own business? Now things are gonna have to get messy."

Eyes wide, Amanda shook her head dramatically. "No. I won't tell anyone I saw you."

The man belched crudely and then issued a loud guffaw before aiming his cold eyes at her again. "You must think we're as dumb as you, Red." He reached out a filthy hand to finger her auburn hair, causing her to shudder in repulsion. Angered, he grasped a fistful of the hair, and with a savage yank, brought her to her knees before releasing it.

Amanda cried out sharply as her captor almost ripped her arms out of their sockets when he forced her to stand again. Under the hostile gazes of the three men, she breathed heavily while trying to tell herself this wasn't really happening. When that didn't work, she altered her train of thought to try to figure out how to escape. But as long as she was being held in a viselike grip, all she could do was try to talk her way out of this mess. *Fine. I'll talk. They'll get so tired of hearing me talk, they'll have to let me go, or go crazy.*

She looked at Kirk for the first time since she'd seen him emerge from the shack. "Kirk, what on earth are you doing here?"

"Playin' checkers, whadaya think?" was the grinning response.

All three men roared with boisterous laughter, and Sneer-face slapped Kirk on the back so hard, he almost fell face-first into the snow. Upon regaining his balance, Kirk glared fiercely at the other man for a tense moment.

Divide and conquer, thought Amanda with glee.

"But Kirk, you're not like these . . . these—" The man holding her, apparently insulted at her implication, jerked her arms, causing her to cry out again. "These men," she finished weakly.

"Ya better keep yer manners, Missy," muttered her captor in a gruff voice.

"Of course." Mustering new spirit, Amanda went on. "I was just telling Kirk I know he's different from some other people. I mean, he helped me move into my house, didn't you, Kirk?'' She waited for the man to nod before going on hopefully. ''Kin, uh, Mr. Russell that is, asked him and Joseph to help me, and they were so kind. They . . . they . . .''

The key. Her eyes widened as she looked at Kirk, who actually had the audacity to almost look embarrassed. His eyes slid away from hers, and he scuffed the toe of his worn work boot in the snow. She gave him a reproachful frown. ''Kirk, you took my spare key, didn't you?''

The rough man's gaze slid momentarily back to her before he returned his concentration to the little pile of snow he was making with his boot.

Obviously growing impatient with all this chitchat, Sneer-face frowned. '' 'Course he did, Red. Keys don't just walk off, ya know.'' His sharp wit elicited more loud laughter from his partners.

''But why?'' Amanda pressed for every extra second of time she could get by continuing to address Kirk. ''I'd only just arrived here. I was no threat to you.''

Kirk shrugged self-consciously. ''Just seemed like a good idea, with you movin' into that house by the airfield an' all.'' Then, with a defensive glare, he pulled himself up straight. ''Turns out I was right, eh? Turns out I had to get into yer house to leave you a little note.''

Her heart in her throat, all Amanda could do was stare back at him in abject terror. These men meant business and the mortal danger she was in suddenly became all too clear. A cold breath of wind whistled around the corner of the shack, but that wasn't what caused her shivers now.

Sneer-face glowered at Kirk and growled, "That's enough explainin'. We got things to take care of."

His dirty hands reached for her and she quickly asked, "But Joseph—he's not involved in this, is he? Did he sabotage the planes?"

Sneer-face spat a stream of tobacco juice into the snow at her feet. "Joseph's too loyal to Russell. Naw, Kirk's handy with tools an' planes. He decided Russell needed somethin' to keep him busy. 'Sides, Joseph's a dry tribe member. Wouldn't be no good to let him in on our little business, right, boys?" He grinned at the others, who agreed with nods and grunts. "An' if you hadn't been so nosy, you wouldn't be in our business, either. You'd be safe an' sound in the arms of your boyfriend."

Amanda fought in vain against the man who still imprisoned her arms. "I was just curious about everything in the village." She felt like she was going to choke. "I wasn't trying to snoop, I swear."

The resigned set to the man's face frightened her even more, and a chill colder than the subzero air swept over her at his next words.

"That's prob'ly true. Sad for you, it don't matter now. You know too much." He looked away, suddenly unable to meet Amanda's eyes. "An' you ain't gettin' in our way." Each word sounded like a rock being tossed into a quarry.

Stall for time, she told herself again. "But why do you do this?"

"Everybody's gotta earn a livin', Red."

Again, Amanda tried to jerk free of her captor, but

he held her so she could barely move at all. Frantically, she tried to reason with Sneer-face, who was obviously the ringleader. "You know, it's not as if you've committed murder. This is just a little thing. I mean, I suppose it's a big deal to the tribe, since it's a violation of rules, but you can't get sent to prison."

An incredulous stare told her he wasn't listening, and her terror grew. "You'll ruin all you've worked for if you hurt me," she added in a rush. "Then you just might go to prison. Think about it."

"We have. That's why we can't let you go. You'll tell Russell."

"No." She shook her head vigorously. "I won't, I promise."

"Liar," he snapped angrily. "Everyone hereabouts knows how you two're thick as thieves. No pun intended," he smirked to the others, who were acting distinctly uncomfortable with the way the interview was progressing. "You'll tell him faster'n snow comes in winter."

Slowly, he shook his head in what appeared to be honest regret. Amanda wanted to scream in terror and frustration at her inability to convince the man to see reason.

"Sorry, Red," he went on. "Wish it didn't have to be this way. But we've worked too hard to let a cheechako get in the way of business." He nodded to his henchmen. "Go ahead."

For the barest moment, the man behind Amanda loosened his grip on her arms and hope leaped in her heart. She struggled valiantly and opened her mouth to scream just before something crashed down on her head. She crumpled into a heap in the cold, crusty snow, lying there in a semiconscious stupor while people talked and a dog barked. The chaos made her head hurt. Closing her eyes eased some of the confusion, and then for some reason, the dog stopped barking.

"... gotta get rid of her ... lousy mutt may bring someone back here," a voice growled. "... do the honors ..."

Kirk guffawed loudly. "... ain't no Lassie, Jack ... too close to town to keep her here. Take her to the dump shack at the halfway point ... fly her out there."

Are they talking about me? The snatches of conversation creeping into Amanda's addled brain were frightening, and she opened her eyes a crack, to see an ugly brown stream of tobacco juice land in the snow next to her shoulder. Stomach churning, she closed her eyes again in disgust.

"... *only* way we can get her out there ... plan on gettin' her to the plane by the lodge without anybody noticin' ... still light ... after dark, by that time the mutt may bring her boyfriend out here ..."

"... want him nosin' around ... suspicious already, an' he'd bring the cops. Probably already found our job on his planes ... load her on the Ski-Doo ... out to the middle of the swamp. Nobody'll find her then."

No! Amanda's mind screamed, but she couldn't muster strength to make a sound. The voices faded in and out, but she forced herself to concentrate.

"Never ..." the voice of Sneer-face interjected,

". . . ever find her bones. Little cheechako just explored too far."

She heard the men roar with heartless laughter until a harsh word from the ringleader silenced them. In panic, Amanda felt herself being lifted, carried, and then deposited on something hard. Mentally, she screamed her head off, but no sound was ever emitted. . . .

With a moan, Amanda weakly lifted one mittened hand to touch the tender bump on her head. She uttered a faint gasp, forced her eyes open, and gazed groggily up at the darkening sky. Stark black spruce trees performed a crazy dance and when she tried to lift her head, there was an explosion of sparks in front of her.

It's so cold. She lay in the snow, trying to focus on the spinning trees. There was a house. And men, one of whom had grabbed her. They'd done this to her, made her head hurt. But something was missing and she looked around in confusion. *The house. Where is it?* A blast of winter wind swept through her clothing, causing her to shudder violently.

It was too quiet. "Frosty. Come here, boy." Fingers of fear crawled up her spine when no wriggling orange bundle approached at her weak plea. Then she remembered his sudden silence during all the confusion, and tears sprang to her eyes, leaving hot trails as they ran down her frozen cheeks.

She sat up slowly. There was just enough pink twilight left to determine in which direction the sun had set. That would be west. Therefore, north lay behind her. She would go north, since the Alcan lay that way. Chena would be between her and the Alcan.

Ever so slowly, she pushed herself up, only to topple back into the snow when her knees buckled. Her head felt as if it was sustaining repeated blows with a hammer, but she was able to recognize the need for some kind of support through the fuzz in her brain. Crawling through the snow to the nearest tree, she grasped it with both hands and pulled herself to a standing position. She clung to the tree until the immediate dizziness had passed and her legs felt more sturdy.

By now it was completely dark, but the moon-washed landscape offered a reflection that enabled her to see quite well. *Start moving. Nobody is going to come and help, because nobody knows where you are. Heck, even* you *don't know where you are.*

She leaned against the tree, forcing her muddled brain to operate. *They talked about a Ski-Doo. There must be tracks in the snow. Find them and follow them back to the shack. It'll be easy to find the road from there.*

Peering narrowly through the moonglow for several minutes, her eyes eventually came to rest on what looked like snowmobile tracks. Following the tracks to civilization made more sense than trying to go north when there was no sun to follow.

A moment of weakness brought a choked sob, and she thought of her father. He had warned her she'd never survive out here in the Alaska bush. His words rang through her aching head, telling her she should stay home where he could protect her, that she was just not made of the strong stuff required to live in isolated and rustic surroundings. Kin shared that opinion. He was still calling her "Princess" despite evidence that she was perfectly capable of handling life out here. He was determined to believe she was just like the woman who had left him at the altar all those years ago.

Well, Amanda Roberts was made of sterner stuff than any of them wanted to believe. She balled her hands into fists inside her snow-encrusted mittens. *I'll show you all I'm no wimp. Somehow, I'll make it through this and stay in Chena. I love the people and the place. One person in particular. . . .* Head pounding, she lurched toward the snowmobile tracks.

An eternity seemed to pass as she waded through the deep snow. Shivering violently from cold, her teeth chattered nonstop even when she clenched them together, making her jaw ache. Plowing on foot through the deep snow was hard work and she became so exhausted she finally decided to allow herself a short rest.

Rest. I just need to lean against this tree and rest. I'm not going to sleep. It's too dangerous in this freezing weather. I've heard people who fall asleep while freezing never wake up. No, she'd just close her eyes and rest for a few minutes before plodding forward. She'd think about Kin's warm, cozy house. His warm, strong arms. . . .

Buzzzzz. The loud sound irritated her, becoming louder still, while she tried to sleep. She curled into a ball to shut out the numbing cold and noise. It worked. The buzzing stopped. Stiff lips curved upward in a soft smile, she marveled at her own cleverness before drifting off again.

Ah, another warm and wonderful dream. Kin held her as he brushed the frost-covered hair from her face. He whispered sweet endearments in her ear, and she smiled. But the dream lost its charm when he started to shake her and speak more loudly. Now what had she done to earn his wrath? When he slapped her cold cheeks, he actually yelled.

"Mandy, sweetheart, wake up. Look at me. Please wake up."

He's begging. Imagine bringing Kincaid Russell to his knees, she thought with a giddy feeling as she snuggled against him. But it didn't feel right. Kin, humbled and begging, was not what she wanted. She loved him just the way he was and only wanted him to return her love. Why was that too much to ask? A miserable whimper escaped her. Still, he continued to shake her.

"Mandy, it's Kin. Wake up, love." He shone a flashlight directly on her face and she opened her eyes to stare stonily into it, not even blinking. To blink would take too much effort. "Oh, Lord, you're really out of it. I've got to get you to shelter."

"Woke me . . . up."

"Mandy, listen to me. You can't sleep. You've got to stay awake."

Amanda allowed her eyes to drift lazily shut. "Don't . . . sleep . . ."

Strong arms swept her up and she felt herself being deposited in a sitting position on something soft. Obviously, Kin wanted to play in the snow. Well, if he wanted to drag her around, that was fine. She giggled in satisfaction. He'd soon tire of this game and let her sleep in peace.

That awful, loud buzzing started again, this time sounding like it was right under her. She sagged against Kin's solid chest as they bounced noisily along. *Are there roller coasters out here?* Just when she was starting to enjoy the jouncing ride, it stopped and Kin spoke to someone else over the din of the idling machine. Then that darn light shone in her face again.

"Exposure," a familiar voice said.

Amanda opened her eyes and looked blearily at Paul. "Gonna play, too?" She offered a crooked smile before drifting back into a stupor.

Paul spoke in a low voice. "... home fast ... called the station on the hand radio to send backup ... shortly ... get moving."

Amanda awoke to find Hailey the Hippo next to her and a robust old Athabascan man holding her wrist to take her pulse. Weak chills quivered through her body and her head pounded mercilessly. "Who ... ?"

The man's eyes were kind as he smiled. "Hello, Amanda. I'm glad you're awake so we can finally meet. I'm Dr. Richards."

Fighting to keep her sleepy eyes open, Amanda saw neat gray hair and wrinkled copper skin. Why was he here? She met his eyes in confusion. "Where are we?"

After patting her hand reassuringly, he tucked it under the covers. "You've had quite an adventure, my dear, but you're going to be fine. You're at Kincaid's house and you're warm and safe. We need to talk about how you're supposed to dress when you go hiking in the Interior in the dead of winter. The first thing you put on is long underwear.'' Brown eyes twinkled as he chided gently.

Embarrassed by her own carelessness, Amanda nodded. ''I was . . . in a hurry.''

The kindly doctor wagged a crooked finger. ''You could have died, my dear. You're suffering from exposure and a nasty bump on the head. Your face was mildly frostbitten but, thanks to Kincaid's quick thinking, it's thawing safely. There should be no damage.''

''Frost . . .'' Amanda struggled against the confines of the blankets. ''I want a mirror,'' she begged. ''I want to see my face.'' In her weakened state, she succeeded only in tangling the covers around herself and soon collapsed in exhaustion. ''Please, help me. A mirror . . .''

The affable doctor handed her a small mirror from his black bag. She grabbed it and held it up to her face in terror, expecting to see black splotches like those which overtook the gangrenous areas that frostbite victims often lost to amputation. All she saw was her own pale face in need of a healthy dose of moisturizer. With a wan smile, she handed the mirror back to Dr. Richards. ''Thank you. Sorry . . . about the panic.''

With an understanding nod, he lay the mirror aside and tucked the blankets more closely about her neck before laying the back of his hand against her forehead. ''Expect a headache and some pain in your arms and legs as you warm up. You became frozen enough that you'll have what we call chilblains. They'll hurt, but you'll be all right. Kincaid knows how to take proper care of you. Stay in bed and follow his instructions.'' He put his stethoscope into his medical bag just as there was a tap at the door. "Come in, Kincaid," he called.

Kin entered the room, a bottle of brandy in his hand. A smile lit his tense features as Amanda wrinkled her nose when she realized his intentions. "Mandy doesn't much like alcohol, Jim, and she probably really hates it after all this mess. But I thought some brandy would help warm her insides."

The kindly doctor responded heartily as he reached for his parka. "An excellent idea, Kincaid. Go ahead and give it to her now."

Though Kin sat on the bed next to her, Amanda refused to meet his eyes. Afraid of her reaction to his touch and hoping to avoid both it and the brandy, she turned her head away.

Sliding a strong arm behind her, he lifted her head and shoulders off the bed, cradling her against his arm. Then he held the bottle to her mouth and coaxed in a warm voice, "Come on, Mandy."

"I don't need—" She was unable to finish her sentence when Kin shoved the bottle against her open lips and poured the amber liquid down her throat. The cutting, vile taste of the stuff served to remind her why she avoided alcohol. With a burning throat and watery eyes, she coughed and twisted away from the bottle. As brandy dribbled down her chin and neck, she sputtered in outrage. "That's awful!"

Kin used a corner of the sheet to dab at the liquid on her skin. "It'll warm your insides, though."

The sudden heat from the brandy coursed through her and Amanda replied, ''On second thought, maybe this booze smuggling isn't such a bad idea.'' She was rewarded with looks of censure from both Kin and the doctor, and had the grace to blush as she tugged at the covers.

After laying her tenderly back against the pillows, Kin pulled the blankets up to her chin. ''Back in a minute,'' he threatened.

Dr. Richards promised to visit Amanda the next day and left the room with Kin. She was glad when they were gone because searing hot knives suddenly slashed through her legs. This was what the doctor had warned her about. She curled up in a ball to counteract the excruciating pain. Tears seeped from her tightly shut eyes and she bit her lower lip.

She felt rather than saw Kin sit on the bed. His strong arms cuddled her and he lay a leathery brown cheek against her pale one.

His voice was kind and soothing. ''You're okay, sweetheart. I know how badly it hurts, but you'll be okay. Thank goodness.''

As the pain eased, she sat up with a grimace. ''What happened to me? I know they hit me on the head, but I was sort of aware of what they were saying and doing. Then I woke up somewhere else. How did you find me?''

A hard look washed over Kin's face and his jet eyes glinted ominously. ''You do remember what happened, then?''

''I'm afraid so,'' she replied in a low voice.

Kin stood restlessly. ''Frosty ran back here. Paul and I had just gotten back from checking on my planes. The dog was so excited, we followed him and he led us to a shack. You weren't there, so we broke in. When we found stores of booze, we knew you'd run into trouble.'' He ran a hand through his hair as he relived the pain of the past few hours. ''We followed their snowmobile tracks and eventually found the smugglers.''

Amanda could barely speak over the lump in her throat. ''Frosty's okay, then?''

''Yeah. We shut him in the storehouse so he wouldn't get into trouble while we looked for you. Paul will bring him home.''

A deep sadness left her. Her dog was okay, and he had helped save her life, bless his fuzzy little heart. He could have scrambled eggs every day for the rest of his life if he wanted.

Kin was pacing, clenched fists causing his knuckles to turn white. ''They refused to tell us what they'd done with you. We cuffed them and Paul stayed to call for backup. I followed more tracks.'' Slamming his fist into his open hand, he continued. ''They'd made circles so finding you would be nearly impossible. When I finally did, you were in bad shape.'' Agony was written on his face as he rejoined her on the bed and took her hand.

Disbelief warred with terror in Amanda's heart. ''They left me out there to die,'' she whispered. Pain shot through her legs just then, bringing more tears to her eyes. She rubbed her legs as hard as she could and gritted her teeth. ''How . . . did I get back here?''

He brushed a strand of tousled hair away from her face. ''I brought you back on the Ski-Doo. You were dead weight and didn't wake up until Jim was examining you."

For the first time, Amanda noticed she was in her nightgown in Kin's bed. Color suffused her cheeks and she pretended great interest in smoothing the blankets over her reclining form. Finally satisfied that there were no unnecessary bumps or creases in the bedcovers, she gazed up at him. "So, did I put this nightie on in my sleep?"

As if to get out of the range of physical violence, Kin stood before answering. "No," he drawled. "I did that. Now before you start yelling, Mandy, you must realize that you were suffering from exposure. And your clothing had frozen with snow and then you were all wet when it melted. There was the risk of hypothermia, so it had to be done quickly. I was the only one here."

"I understand. Thanks."

With a relieved smile, he sidled closer again. "I've heated some soup, and hot water for herbal tea. If you promise not to go for any long walks, I'll go to the kitchen and get them."

Her face contorted with the pain in her legs. "I don't think I'll be doing any hiking just yet."

She rubbed her legs and smiled wanly as he nodded in sympathy and left the room. Falling back against the pillows, she thought about her ordeal and said a little prayer of thanks for her safe deliverance from the clutches of the smugglers and a freezing death.

The doorbell rang as she pushed back the covers and swung her feet to the floor, stifling a groan when they made painful contact with the solid surface. Kin's maroon velour robe hung on a hook in the closet and she pulled it on over her gown as Paul's voice and Frosty's excited barks carried down the hall. She was rolling up the dangling sleeves when Frosty bounded into the room, followed by Kin, Paul, and more excruciating pain shooting through her legs.

Kin thrust a tray of soup, crackers, and tea into Paul's hands. He loomed over Amanda, who knelt on the floor, hugging herself, her face buried in her lap while she rode out the pain. Frosty whimpered and tried to bathe her ear, since that was the only skin he could contact with his long, pink tongue.

"Mandy, what are you doing out of bed?" Kin stroked her bowed back until the waves of pain passed, then unceremoniously scooped her up in his arms and placed her on the bed. "And in bare feet, no less."

"I felt like getting up for a little while and my robe and slippers aren't in here," she defended herself, feeling somewhat breathless after the trauma. She looked over Kin's shoulder as he tucked her back under the covers, robe and all. "Hi, Paul."

Relief was evident on the trooper's face. "Hi, Amanda. You were chilled pretty bad, and Kin's right. You've got to stay warm." He inclined his head toward the dog. "I sprung Frosty from the prison we put him in earlier."

Looking guiltily at Kin with soulful brown eyes, her ecstatic mutt proceeded to jump up on the bed and curl close to his mistress. At Kin's chuckle, his scraggly tail thumped the bedcovers twice, and he lay his soft head on Amanda's lap in pure contentment.

"I'm on my way to the station to book those guys," Paul said. "Dennis and John showed up as backup and went on ahead with them.'' He set the soup tray on the nightstand. ''Amanda, if you'll come by the station tomorrow, you can press charges.''

Amanda became very still. ''Against all of them?''

Both men frowned at her, and Paul replied, ''Of course. We got them both.''

''Both? You got two?''

Paul's eyes met Kin's before he turned his gaze back to Amanda, a cautious look in his eyes. ''Yes, two. There were two men, right?''

With a heavy sigh, Amanda lay her head back against the pillows. ''I don't know how to tell you this.'' Her voice cracked as she spoke to Kin. ''I suppose he was your friend.''

He looked horrified at her cryptic words. ''Who? Tell us, please.''

''Kirk,'' she said quietly, pushing on despite their audible gasps. ''He's one of the smugglers. He was the one who took my spare house key. And he later went in to leave the note.''

Paul sagged against the wall while Kin sat down hard on the bed next to her. ''I can't believe it. One of the locals,'' Kin murmured.

''I'm sorry.''

Paul straightened and said curtly, ''I'd better go. I have a criminal to round up. He's probably at home.''

When he was gone, Kin stood to get the tray Paul had set on the nightstand, and returned to the bed. ''You've got to stay in bed and keep warm tonight,'' he chided her, spooning some of the aromatic soup into her mouth.

Amanda pinned him with a direct gaze and took the spoon from him. ''Fine. But I can feed myself.''

She took the tray from him. "And I wish you'd talk to me. I know you probably never expected a villager to actually be one of the smugglers."

Kin ran a hand through his hair, rubbed his neck, and shook his head in sadness. "I don't know. I guess I knew it was a possibility."

"I know he's not Athabascan, but I suppose that doesn't help."

"No. He's been in Chena for twenty-odd years. Who'd have thought he'd prey on people by smuggling booze?"

They were silent for a while, each contemplating the weaknesses that cause people to do wrong. Kin was first to recover his usual spirit as he placed his hands on his hips.

"Eat. The nightmare is over and they're all going to pay. Case closed."

Since he'd made it clear he didn't want to talk about Kirk or the smuggling anymore, Amanda changed the subject. "I don't see why I need to stay in your bed. At least allow me to go into my own room while I stay at your house. Which, by the way, need only be until tomorrow. I can go home now that the smugglers have been caught."

Kin reached to pat Frosty. "You can stay in here tonight."

Amanda carefully lifted another spoonful of the hot soup. "You make a mean chicken soup."

"Well, it's sort of . . . canned," he admitted.

Mischief glimmered in her eyes, and she grinned. "You did a good job of heating it." Her gaze strayed to a collection of photos on his dresser. There was a family photo that included Chief Chena, and her heart plummeted. Some problems had been solved, while others still remained.

Abruptly, she pushed the tray away. "I think I'll go to sleep now. And I'll be out of here tomorrow." She snuggled down under the blankets as Kin picked up the tray.

"Mandy, there's no hurry. I want you to stay here."

But she had already closed her eyes and pretended to be too tired to respond. Her tears were hidden when she turned away from him, curling into a ball once more. This time, the pain shot through her heart as well as her legs, and it felt much worse than those that had gone before.

Chapter Ten

When Amanda awoke, the luminous hands on the bedside clock indicated it was six-thirty in the morning. She had slept for nearly twelve hours. Daylight wouldn't break for many hours yet. A fully dressed Kin was asleep in one of the overstuffed armchairs by the window. She realized he must have slept there all night, and her heart burst with tenderness.

A good night's sleep had worked wonders and she was feeling much more positive this morning. Chief Chena would have to come around if Kin was as serious about her as she was about him.

After pushing back the covers, she slid quietly out of the big bed and, with Frosty in tow, crept from the room, closing the heavy door behind her. Back in her own room, she dressed and finished gathering her belongings. It seemed an age had passed since she had begun packing yesterday after discovering her water pipes weren't frozen.

The note she left for Kin on the kitchen counter, thanking him for his hospitality and kindness, seemed stilted and formal. But how did one explain one's feelings in a note without being certain just how far those feelings were returned? At least she would leave his house with some remnants of pride. There would be time later to find out where he stood. In the meantime, she needed to be alone to think.

With dog and belongings in her car, she drove away, past the A-frame, and out to the Alaska State Troopers' station on the highway. Since Paul was off duty, another officer helped file a report and complaint, charging the smugglers with aggravated assault and attempted murder.

Back in her car outside the police station, Amanda absently gnawed a thumbnail and tried to decide what to do next. It was certain that Kin, when he awoke, would go to the A-frame and try to question her about the abrupt departure. She'd rather not face him until she felt better prepared to deal with his cross-examination and the possibility that he was serious about her. Because if he was, he was going to have to change his way of thinking about cheechakos. A leisurely drive to Tok was the only clear avenue of escape. By the time she got back, Kin would surely have given up and gone to work at one of his places of business.

It wasn't long before she discovered she hadn't missed much on her first trip to Tok. It was a small town, bigger than Chena, but not big enough to hold any major attractions. The hour was too early for the local movie house or to explore what passed for the Tok Mall.

She browsed in the grocery store to kill time, picking up a few items that Kin's store didn't have and that she'd been unable to purchase last time due to limited space on the sled. Walking Frosty in the bitter cold caused her fingers and toes to tingle and hurt. *Probably because I nearly froze to death yesterday.* Such an experience would certainly sensitize one's limbs and appendages for a while. It was still early in the day when she headed slowly back to Chena.

Kin's Blazer was parked at the general store so she felt no qualms about going home. Of course, it was for the best that he wasn't at her house, but she couldn't avoid feeling a pang of disappointment. Deep inside, she had hoped he'd be waiting for her, despite the vehement denials.

It wasn't until she had set the groceries in the kitchen and was heading toward the stairs with her suitcase that she noticed the fire burning cheerfully in the woodstove. Kincaid Russell watched her from a comfortable position on the overstuffed couch.

" 'Bout time you came back," he said mildly.

Amanda hesitated, considering flight instead of dealing with him now. Maybe she'd wanted him to be waiting, but it would have been nice to be prepared, all the same. Giving herself a mental shake, she straightened her spine and set the suitcase on the floor. She was stronger than she had ever been and able to handle whatever he wanted to dish out. Anyone who could undergo what she had yesterday, and then be running around shopping today, had plenty of staying power and fortitude. A satisfied smile turned up the corners of her mouth.

She felt a new and powerful self-confidence. "How long have you been waiting for me?"

"All my life."

The world tilted ominously, and her mouth felt dry while she digested his words.

Kin rose and took her hand, guiding her to the couch. "I think it's time we discussed it. Don't you?"

An involuntary leap of her heart caused her voice to rattle thinly. "I thought you were at the store."

Kin helped her out of her coat before she sat warily down on the couch next to him. When she tried to move strategically away, he placed a green wool-clad arm snugly around her shoulders.

His thumb stroked her cheek. "That was my plan," he said shamelessly. "You were avoiding me. Trickery was necessary."

"Why would I avoid you?" she demanded with a spirited toss of her head.

"You tell me. Could it be you're afraid of your feelings for me?"

An unladylike snort was her defense. "Now you're trying to psychoanalyze me? You're wrong, *Doctor* Russell. I'm not afraid of anything. Not anymore—"

The brave words were smothered on her lips as he warmly pressed his own against them. Instinctively she responded with all the love she felt for him, and his arms tightened around her.

When he pulled his mouth reluctantly away from hers, his voice was hoarse. "Can you imagine what life together would be like for us? The fun and excitement—"

"I don't know if I can handle all the fun and excitement in this town." She liked the way the conversation was beginning, but his proximity played havoc with her senses and she pushed against his iron chest.

"I'd say you handle it very well."

"Besides," she said in a huff, "you've got another woman on your line already."

Viselike arms sprang open in shock and he gaped at her, slack-jawed, before hooting with laughter. When she stood in disgust, he grabbed her hands and pulled her back down next to him.

Gaining control of his mirth, he contemplated her wide, flashing eyes. "You're jealous. I don't know why, but you're jealous of somebody." He let out a whoop of glee. "Boy, I sure got lucky the day you nearly ran me off that bridge."

"I am not jealous! And I didn't run you off—"

Ignoring her protest, he smiled in remembrance. "You were so determined to show me how tough you were. And I was just as determined to chase you away. I didn't want any more cheechakos hurting me." His callused hand cupped her cheek and his eyes softened. "But you stormed your way into my heart with your artless, outspoken ways and your stubbornness. You're so naive, you sent me mixed signals, welcoming me one minute and pushing me away the next. I wanted to believe that innocence was real.

It's so unusual these days. But I thought you were playing games. Now I find out you're actually jealous."

Dreading the hope burgeoning within her heart, Amanda was barely able to whisper, "Shouldn't I be? I mean, isn't Lucinda sort of special to you?"

"No. We're lifelong friends. Period. She has nothing to do with us. I thought I told you that before."

Us. He said us. Gazing into the depths of his eyes, she saw only truth and openness. "No, you never told me that," she mocked. "But you'd better tell Elly that." A slight frown marred her smooth forehead. "Didn't you give her a ring yesterday?"

Kin looked appalled. "Elly? Certainly not," he responded indignantly. A slap on his shoulder from a giggling Amanda caused him to hold up his hands in surrender. "A ring for Lucy? What made you think that, anyway?"

Amanda looked down at her hands. "I heard her tell you it was a beautiful ring when she was leaving yesterday." She took a deep breath. "And I thought you might have a ring box in your shirt pocket when we were . . . kissing," she finished weakly.

The look of dawning amazement on his face told her everything was becoming clear. "Oh, my love. You thought I was engaged to Elly? I mean Lucy?" His eyes danced happily.

All she could think was that he had called her "my love!"

Bells of happiness rang and it took great self-control not to fling her arms around him in joy. But her hands gripped each other tightly in her lap while she awaited his further explanation.

Kin's eyes glowed with an inner fire as his own hands entwined with hers. "Amanda Roberts, I love you with every fiber of my being. That's what I told Lucy yesterday. And"—he paused and reached into the pocket of his coat, which lay on the end of the couch, to withdraw a small, black velvet box, opening

it to display a sparkling diamond and sapphire ring—
"I showed her this. I told her I bought it in Anchorage
and hoped you would wear it one day. She wished us
the best."

He heaved a sigh and his head fell back against the
couch, his twinkling eyes shifting to her face.
"Mandy, Lucy is like my own sister. We're very
close. That's the only reason I told her about it."

Tears spilled unchecked down Amanda's cheeks.
After all the pain, all her efforts to prove herself to
him, to find out he loved her all along. He'd had this
ring before they even went to Tok. "I can't believe
this is happening," she cried, choking on a sob of
joy.

Kin cuddled her close and ran a gentle hand down
her hair. "Believe it, sweetheart. There will never be
anyone for me but you."

Sniffling, she clung to him, and buried her face in
his warm shoulder. Her nostrils were tickled by min-
gled scents of pine needles and woodsmoke.

" 'Course, I don't know how I'm going to break
the news to Elly . . ." Laughter rumbled through his
chest.

Amanda pulled away with an indignant huff. "I
didn't ever think you were involved with Elly. That
was your little joke."

Obviously enjoying her vexation, he proffered a
cheerful leer. "You think Elly dreams about me as
much as I dream about you?" He watched the color
flare in her cheeks. "I love you, Mandy. And I swear,
you are the toughest cheechako lady I've ever known.
Not that it matters. I can't live without you, however
weak or strong you may be."

Then his hands came up to cradle her face and he spoke very seriously. "But you've shown such strength and fortitude since you've been here. The isolation and cold, the darkness, none of those things seem to bother you. And the way you worked up a sweat right alongside me when we were trying to open the gate for the team at George's house . . . well, that's true pioneer spirit. Being cold and tired and hungry, and forging ahead with the manual labor that needs to be done before seeking comfort."

"So I passed all your tests?"

"There weren't any tests, Mandy. I tried to think in terms of testing, but I was really just observing. With my heart," he explained with deep feeling. "To protect myself from pain like I experienced before."

"I love you," she blurted.

Fortunately, she was already close, because Kin's large hands reached out to drag her onto his lap. She wrapped her arms contentedly around him and closed her eyes to shut out all sensations except the solid feel and woodsy scent of him. His heart beat steadily where her head lay against his chest and she smiled as peace washed over her.

"What about your grandfather?" she asked dreamily.

"Mmm. Let him get his own girl." He yelped when she playfully tugged a lock of his hair. "Really, he's only concerned about you running off and leaving me because you can't cut it out here. You're young and a cheechako and he's sure you'll head for the Lower Forty-eight at the first sign of hardship."

"Just like you."

"Wrong. I know better, and he soon will." He nuzzled her earlobe and she turned her face up for his kiss.

"Kin?" she ventured softly a short time later.

"Hmm?"

"How long do I have to live here before I'm not a cheechako?"

"Oh, for most people it takes about twenty years to shed the title. But for you, I'd say forever." He slanted a smile at the woman in the crook of his arm. "What about it? Think you can stay in Chena for the rest of your life?"

"Depends on the deal I'm offered," she replied with a coquettish bat of her lashes.

His eyes lingered on her lips and his voice was low and throaty. "How about lifetime partner to your favorite Athabascan? Will you marry me?"

She smiled happily as he slid the glistening circle of white gold set with a diamond and sapphires on her finger. "Yes. I'll marry you. As long as I don't have to wait too long."

"Will three days be too long? We can get the license in Tok today and your family can fly into Anchorage and drive up here in time for the wedding. Your father can see what a real 'sourdough' his little girl has become. Wait till he hears that you solved Chena's smuggling mystery and lived to tell about it." His eyes gleamed wickedly. "But you have to promise me one thing."

"What?"

He was as solemn as she had ever seen him. "That the honeymoon will last forever."

Love shone on Amanda's face when she looked into his liquid eyes, eyes in which she thought she would drown. She wanted to, forever. Glorying in his warm embrace, she sank backward into the cushions.

"Oh, I don't think that will be a problem, my love. No problem at all," she murmured, surrendering to her heart's desire.